THE ÉMIGRÉS

THE ÉMIGRÉS

CARL RICHARDSON

Matador
9 Priory Business Park,
Wistow Road, Kibworth Beauchamp,
Leicestershire. LE8 0RX
Tel: 0116 279 2299
Email: books@troubador.co.uk
Web: www.troubador.co.uk/matador
Twitter: @matadorbooks

ISBN 978 1800460 706

British Library Cataloguing in Publication Data.
A catalogue record for this book is available from the British Library.

Printed on FSC accredited paper
Printed and bound in Great Britain by 4edge Limited
Typeset in 11pt Minion Pro by Troubador Publishing Ltd, Leicester, UK

Matador is an imprint of Troubador Publishing Ltd

Born and brought up in West Cumbria Carl Richardson studied at Manchester Polytechnic and Newcastle University. He spent most of his working life as a civil servant. Now retired, he lives in Cumbria and writes novels in his retirement.

Cover image: Carlisle Citadel
Photo by the author

One

London, Tuesday 22ⁿᵈ August 1939

The bells of St Clement Danes Church were sounding the quarter hour for a quarter past midday when Robert Aldcroft walked across the Strand and into Essex Street. Fifty yards down the street, he climbed the steps to the entrance to Ridley and Cooper, chartered accountants, who occupied the ground floor of a tall, narrow, mid-terrace building. He rang the bell, and after a minute the door was opened by a young man in a well-pressed suit.

"Yes, can I help?"

"I was hoping to see Mr Harvey, George Harvey, if he's free. My name's Robert Aldcroft. He's not expecting me, but it's a matter of some importance."

"Mr Harvey's with a client at the moment, but I expect he'll be taking his lunch shortly, if you'd care to wait."

"I'd be grateful if you could let him know that I'm here."

The young man showed Aldcroft to a small waiting room, where he sat down. After ten minutes or so, he heard voices outside. He recognised George Harvey's voice – he was evidently taking leave of his client. A few moments later, Harvey appeared in the doorway of the waiting room. He looked surprised.

"I thought…" he began.

"Come in and close the door."

George Harvey did so.

"I thought the rule was that members of the group were not supposed to be seen together in public," Harvey said.

"I know, but this is an emergency. I've got some bad news." Aldcroft paused. "I hardly know where to begin. The crisis is upon us. There will be war in the next two or three days. We've received information, which is being treated as reliable, that the Germans will attack Poland this weekend. Parliament is being recalled for an emergency session tomorrow to pass a national security Act. I'm not sure what it will be called, but it will allow the authorities to round up and detain, without trial, anyone they don't like. The Act will come into force as soon as it's passed tomorrow. That's the reason I'm here now. I've been shown a list of people who are going to be detained under the Act. I can't say by whom, for obvious reasons, but I have every reason to believe that the list is genuine. As well as many other names, I saw that it contained the names of several members of our group, National Renaissance. I had to memorise the names. I couldn't write them down – again, for obvious reasons.

2

As well as you and Christine, there was Geoff and Sylvia, Graham, and also me."

George Harvey sat down on one of the waiting room chairs, as if he suddenly needed support.

"Arrested? We're going to be arrested?"

"Arrested – detained – I'm not sure what they'll call it. But it won't be like a conventional arrest, where you're charged pending a trial. There won't be any trials. People will just be arrested and locked up, presumably for the duration of the war. According to what I've been told, the Act they're going to rush through Parliament tomorrow will suspend civil liberties – suspend *Habeas Corpus*. It'll give the authorities the power of arbitrary arrest and detention without trial."

"Then… in that case, their moral bankruptcy is finally complete. As well as wanting to be warmongers, they want to be dictators as well. What are we to do?"

"There isn't a lot of choice. If we stay, we'll be rounded up and interned. The alternatives are to go into hiding, or leave the country."

"Leave the country?"

"It may sound daunting, but I think it's the best option. Going into hiding might sound easier, but you'd be committing yourself to the life of a fugitive, either constantly on the run, or constantly in fear of discovery and arrest. It'd be difficult to lead a civilised existence because you'd always have to be ready to flee at a moment's notice. Leaving the country is the only safe option. I don't know if you knew, but Mike Warren has a house in Dublin, which he bought last year for just this eventuality. Mike's name

3

wasn't on the list I saw, but that doesn't mean he isn't in danger. I'm going to contact Mike this afternoon to warn him of what's happening, but also to ask if he'd be prepared to put up temporarily those of us whose names are on the list, until we can arrange alternative accommodation in Dublin."

"Dublin? Would we be safe there?"

"Yes, I think so. I had a conversation with Mike when he told me about his house there, and he said that there's no chance that the Irish would extradite anyone to Britain for political reasons. Not after all that's happened in the last twenty years or so. So, we'll be as safe there as anywhere."

"I see. How much time have we got?"

"To be honest, none at all. They're going to rush this Act through Parliament tomorrow, which means that it'll be on the Statute Book by the end of the day. That means that they could start making arrests as early as tomorrow evening. Those of us who are on the list at least, need to go as soon as possible."

George Harvey was silent for a moment before speaking.

"I suppose it's not entirely unexpected, given the nature of the political situation. We already have to take precautions in case the authorities take action against us. One always hoped that it would never happen, even while knowing that it's an ever-present danger. But it's still a shock, now that it's happened. Suddenly to have to pack one's whole life up, with scarcely any time to think. It's hard to come to terms with. I mean, what about my position here at the firm if I just leave without warning?"

Robert Aldcroft shook his head.

"That's the wrong way of looking at it. Your name was on that list. If you do nothing, you'll be interned, possibly as early as tomorrow evening. That would certainly end your position here. If you keep your freedom by leaving the country, then you maintain at least the possibility of salvaging something eventually. Once you're locked up in Wormwood Scrubs or wherever they incarcerate political prisoners, there'll be no possibility of salvaging anything."

"Yes, I see. Dublin. We must go to Dublin tomorrow?"

"No later than tomorrow. You, Christine and the children as well. Christine's name was also on the list."

"So you said. Dublin. The boat train for Ireland goes from Euston, doesn't it?"

"Yes, but there may not be enough time for that. It's a measure of the urgency of the situation. My recommendation is that you travel by aeroplane."

"Aeroplane! I've never flown before."

"I think it's the only way you're going to be sure of getting out in time. I've gathered a bit of information together and jotted it down." He handed George Harvey a piece of paper. "There are two flights a day from Croydon to Dublin, flown by the Irish airline Aer Lingus. They don't have an office in London for some reason, so you have to book tickets through other airlines, which act as agents. You should book through the Dutch airline KLM. They have an office on Horseferry Road. Don't book through Imperial Airways, or any British airline. They may pass information about passenger bookings on to the authorities. KLM isn't likely to do that. I've booked tickets for Mary and myself for tomorrow afternoon's flight. The morning flight tomorrow is already fully booked, but there are still seats available on the afternoon flight. I advise you to do that now, without delay. I can't overstate the urgency of the matter."

"Yes, I understand. And thank you for coming to tell me. If we need to let everyone know, I could contact Geoff and Sylvia and Elizabeth this afternoon, if that would help."

"Yes, I'd be grateful if you could. I'm going to speak to Mike Warren and Duncan Watkinson this afternoon. Duncan's the only person who will be able to contact Graham Shepherd in time, so it's important I speak to him."

"What about trying to contact him by telephone?"

Robert Aldcroft shook his head.

"I don't want to break the rule about telephones, even in this situation. As long as I can speak to Duncan this afternoon, I'm confident we can warn Graham in time."

"I hope so. Well, I'm not sure when I'll see you again, so thank you and good luck."

Robert Aldcroft stood up, preparing to leave.

"If you manage to book tomorrow afternoon's flight, I'll see you at Croydon. Good luck!"

After Robert Aldcroft had left, George Harvey went back to his office and sat down at his desk. For a minute he just sat there, taking in what he had just been told. He needed a few minutes to think about what he was going to do. He looked at his appointments book, to see what appointments he had that afternoon and on the morrow.

He had two appointments that afternoon, the first at 2pm, the second at 2.45; so he should be free from 3.30pm at the latest. Tomorrow, he had three appointments in the morning and two in the afternoon. He looked at the piece of paper that Robert Aldcroft had given him. The afternoon flight tomorrow left Croydon at 3.30pm, with passengers being picked up from a collection point on Lower Belgrave Street an hour earlier. Timing was now going to be important. A few minutes later he left the building and walked up to the Strand, where he caught a bus going down to Whitehall.

On leaving the offices of Ridley and Cooper, Robert Aldcroft continued walking down Essex Street, cut through to Temple Place, and went down into Temple Underground station. Fifteen minutes later he emerged from South Kensington Underground station, crossed to Brompton Road and turned into Glendower Place. He walked up to the entrance to the offices of Duncan Watkinson LL.D. (Oxon), solicitor. He was in luck. Duncan Watkinson was in, and when news about his visitor was passed to him, he immediately asked for Robert Aldcroft to be ushered through to his office.

"This is unexpected," he said.

"I have some bad news, and the matter is urgent." As briefly as he could, Robert Aldcroft explained about the impending Act of Parliament, and the list he had seen. "Several members of National Renaissance are on the list, including myself," he continued. "I've managed to have warnings sent to all those whose names are on the list except Graham Shepherd. Your name isn't on the list, but

I was hoping that you would be able to drive out to Essex this afternoon or this evening to warn Graham."

"I see. This is something of a shock. Yes, I'll certainly drive out to speak to Graham this evening. But wouldn't it be quicker to telephone?"

"I don't want to break the rule about using the telephone, even now. Perhaps especially now, as I expect the authorities are listening in all the time."

"You say that your name is on this list. Why would that be? You haven't been engaging openly in political activity like some of us."

"I suspect it's because of what I know because of my work at the Foreign Office. Basically, I know too much. People who know too much are potentially dangerous; and if they're politically unreliable, then they're definitely dangerous. I have to say that I wasn't all that surprised to see my name on the list, although it was still a shock."

"What are you going to do?"

"I'm making arrangements to travel to Dublin."

"Dublin – will you be safe there?"

"Yes. The Irish won't extradite anyone to Britain for political reasons, so I'm advising everyone whose name is on the list to make their way to Dublin as soon as possible. That's the main message I want you to give to Graham when you speak to him this evening."

"Yes, I see. What about your wife, Mary?"

"I haven't had a chance to speak to Mary yet. I only found out about all this earlier today. But Mary and I will go to Dublin together. The last thing she would want is to be stuck in a war of Chamberlain's making."

"Of course, I understand."

"What will you do yourself?" asked Aldcroft.

"You say my name isn't on this list?"

"No. I went right through it, and your name wasn't there. That doesn't mean you aren't in danger. I'm letting everyone in the group know, whether their name's on the list or not. Obviously, those whose names are on the list need to leave as soon as possible, and I'm advising people to make for Dublin as the safest place to go."

"I will probably follow you in due course. But if my name isn't on the list, it gives me time to put my affairs in order here first. Not being able to do that must be a daunting prospect – suddenly having to leave everything behind."

Robert Aldcroft shrugged.

"When the alternative is to be sent to prison indefinitely, there isn't much choice. We'll do what we can under the circumstances. I haven't had much time to think about it, but if possible I'll appoint an agent to look after the house until it becomes clearer what the outlook is. My main concern now is to make sure that everyone is warned of the danger in time."

"Well, I appreciate your coming to warn me. And I shall certainly speak to Graham. If you're going to Dublin straight away, I'm not sure when I'll see you again."

"Well, if you follow, I'll see you in Dublin."

"Yes, of course. How will I contact you?"

"I don't have a settled address there at the moment. Obviously, I haven't had time to arrange anything. When you arrive, if we're still not in contact, the best thing to do would be to put a notice in the personal column of *The Irish Times*. We'll be watching for it, and we'll contact you."

"I shall remember that. Well, good luck!"

They shook hands.

"Good luck!"

Two

A few minutes after noon on the following day, Robert Aldcroft left the Foreign Office building on King Charles Street. It would almost certainly be the last time he would ever be in the building where he had worked for most of his career as a civil servant, and he paused for a minute, looking back into the grand entrance hall for a last memory of it, before stepping out into the street. He turned right into Parliament Street and walked down to the taxi rank there. He leaned in to explain to the driver of the leading taxi what he wanted, before climbing into the back of the vehicle. The driver was more than agreeable – this was going to be a big fare.

Aldcroft's first stop was at his bank, where he withdrew £200 in cash, and made arrangements for money to be transferred to the bank's Dublin branch. The next stop was at an estate agent's office, which he had selected after a perusal of a business directory the previous evening. After confirming that they offered the management of property in the owner's absence, he wrote down some details and said that he would contact them again in the near future about a specific property he would like them to manage.

Back in the taxi, they set off for Aldcroft's home in Chiswick. On arrival, he told the taxi to wait. His wife Mary had been busy that morning. She had obtained a couple of packing cases from a local removals firm, and had packed as much as she could of their most valued possessions into them. One of them, containing a lot of books, was now rather heavy. She had gone round the house making sure that all the windows were closed and locked, and that the house was safe to be left unoccupied for an extended period. She had everything ready by the time Robert Aldcroft arrived. The two packing cases were loaded onto the taxi, the heavier one beside the driver, while he and Aldcroft lifted the lighter one onto the taxi's roof rack. Mary had also packed two small suitcases. She and Robert spent a couple of minutes walking through all the rooms of the house, taking a last look round. They might never see the house again.

Within fifteen minutes of Aldcroft's arrival they were on their way. They drove back into Westminster, crossed the river over Vauxhall Bridge, drove past The Oval cricket ground, turned onto Brixton Road and continued on down to Croydon. Finally, in South Croydon, the taxi turned off Purley Way into the entrance to the London Airport.

The taxi driver evidently knew the routine at the airport. He went with Aldcroft to the office of the agents for Aer Lingus and obtained a luggage trolley from them, which he pushed back to the taxi. He and Aldcroft loaded the packing cases and suitcases onto the trolley and pushed it back to the agents' office. They returned to the taxi, where Aldcroft thanked the driver and paid him his fare, which was a generous one. Robert and Mary then returned to the agents' office. As Robert had been advised when he had booked the tickets the previous day, they would only be allowed to take the two small suitcases onto the aeroplane. However, the two packing cases could be forwarded to Dublin as freight by sea, and Robert made arrangements for that. They would be forwarded to the Aer Lingus freight depot at Baldonnel airport in Dublin, where Robert would collect them.

It was now just after 2pm, and as neither of them had had any lunch, they went into the airport restaurant. This was a long, narrow room with a counter down one side and a line of small, square tables along the other. They ordered hot Cornish pasties, scones and a pot of tea. Neither of them spoke much. They were both feeling the stress of the situation. A roar of engines outside announced the arrival of an aeroplane, and after they had finished eating, they went out to the viewing area where people could sit and watch the aircraft. Several aircraft were parked on the tarmac. The aircraft that had just arrived, an Air France Bloch 220, was now disembarking passengers who were walking over to the terminal building. Other passengers were walking out to an elegant DH.91 monoplane of Imperial Airways, while to the left, a KLM DC-3 was being refuelled. Also visible were two DH.86 biplanes, one of which, Aldcroft realised in a moment of excitement, was their own aircraft. He pointed it out to Mary, who looked at it with interest. Further away, on the edge of the tarmac, was the angular shape of a Ju 52 3m of Deutsche Lufthansa.

They sat and watched as the Imperial Airways DH.91 started its engines one by one, and after taxiing out onto the field, it took off and climbed slowly into the sky to the south. A few minutes later, a DH.89 Rapide landed and taxied towards them onto the tarmac. A group of passengers walked out and boarded the Air France Bloch, and they watched while its engines started and it taxied out and took off.

Robert looked at his watch. It was now after 3pm. He touched Mary on the arm, indicating it was time to go. They got up and walked back into the main hall. As they did so, a group of people walked in through the main entrance. The bus carrying the passengers for the Aer Lingus flight had arrived. They quickly recognised Geoff and Sylvia Greenwood, and George and Christine Harvey and their two children, Barbara, aged five, and Angela, aged seven. Recognition was mutual, and they greeted each other.

"Did you speak to Elizabeth?" Robert asked George Harvey.

George nodded and looked around before saying in a low voice: "I told her what you said, and she said she would travel to Dublin as a precaution; but she said she didn't like the idea of flying, so she's travelling on today's boat train."

"That might be risky if the boat doesn't leave until tonight."

"I said that to her, but that's what she's decided to do. She said she would try and book into the Shelbourne Hotel on St Stephen's Green. Apparently she's been there before."

"I see." Robert was thoughtful. "Have you heard anything from Graham?" he asked.

George shook his head. "Did you manage to speak to Duncan?"

"Yes, yesterday lunchtime. However, he may not have been able to drive out to speak to Graham until the evening. It's a long drive."

"Well, that might explain why he isn't here. We were only able to book tickets because they agreed to let the children share our seats. Barbara will be sitting with me, and Angela with Christine. I think the aeroplane's fully booked up."

"We may not be the only ones trying to escape. I managed to speak to Mike yesterday, and he said he'll be coming over to Dublin in a few days to unlock his house there. It's closed up at the moment as he hasn't used it much this season. He said he'll be able to put us up in the short-term until we can find somewhere permanent to live."

"That's kind of him," said George. "Permanent?" he added after a pause.

"If there is a war, I think it'll be a long war, and we certainly won't be able to go back until after the war's over, if even then. So effectively, yes it will be permanent."

They followed the rest of the group over to the departure gate where the Aer Lingus stewardess was waiting to collect the passengers for her aircraft.

"If everyone can have their tickets ready, please," she said when they were all assembled. "Can you please put your hand luggage onto the scales as I check your ticket."

She checked off everyone's ticket one by one, ticking the names on her copy of the passenger list, and noting the readings from the scales by each name.

"Right, that's everyone." She glanced at her watch. As she did so, there was the sound of an aircraft starting its engines just outside. The KLM DC-3 was preparing to depart. The stewardess waited until it had run up its engines and taxied out onto the field to take off.

"Right, if everyone can follow me, please." She led the way out through the gate. Outside, the two nearest aircraft on the tarmac were both four-engined DH.86s. The nearer one was the Railway Air Services flight to Glasgow. Just beyond it was their own aircraft, white painted, with its registration EI-ABK painted in large black letters along its side. The stewardess stood by the steps up to the passenger door, checking them off as they climbed up into the aircraft. There were seven pairs of seats with a central aisle. Robert and Mary were sat side by side across the aisle. Geoff was in the seat behind Sylvia, while George and Christine were having to sit separately in different parts of the cabin, each sitting with one of the children. As they were settling into their seats, the door at the front of the passenger cabin opened, and the pilot emerged from the control cabin. He conferred with the stewardess, who showed him the passenger list. He scrutinised this for a minute before nodding and returning to the control cabin, closing the door behind him. The stewardess closed the passenger door and then walked up to the front of the cabin.

"Will everyone please fasten their seat belts as soon as the aeroplane's engines start," she announced. "Please also remember the rule about no smoking during takeoff and landing. I'll let you know when you can unfasten your seat belts."

She walked back and took her seat at the back of the cabin. The aircraft's engines started one by one, the pilot running them up in preparation for takeoff. They were very noisy – Robert noticed little Barbara, sitting beside George Harvey, putting her fingers in her ears in response. George looked a little nervous. The other DH.86 had already taken off, so once the passenger steps and wheel chocks had been pulled away, the pilot released the brakes and taxied off the tarmac and onto the field, going straight into the takeoff run. The aircraft bumped over the grass surface, swaying slightly as it did so. The tail lifted, and then they were airborne, climbing away slowly. As it flew over the rooftops of Purley, the aircraft began to turn, still climbing, until it was flying west into the sun. For the next forty minutes they cruised above south Berkshire and north Wiltshire, and a green mosaic of fields and hedges. Looking at such peaceful countryside, it was hard to believe that war was so close, and that they were having to flee for their liberty.

At length, the stewardess made her way to the front of the cabin to announce that they would shortly be landing at Bristol, and everyone should fasten their seat belts and extinguish any cigarettes. Robert saw no sign of Bristol before they arrived. There were just green fields and areas of woodland, and then they were landing. The wheels bumped over the grass as the aircraft taxied up to the long single-storey airport terminal building. 'Bristol Airport' was painted in very large letters on the side of an adjoining hangar. This was effectively the last opportunity the authorities would have to apprehend them, and Robert kept a watchful eye open for any sign of trouble. After the engines stopped, the co-pilot emerged into the passenger cabin and conferred with the stewardess. Passenger steps were wheeled up to the aircraft, and the stewardess then opened the passenger door, descended the steps and walked over to the airport building. A few minutes later she returned, accompanied by two people, a man and a woman, each carrying a small suitcase. Robert looked at them with interest as they approached. For a moment he wondered if they were Graham and Ann Shepherd, somehow joining the aircraft at Bristol; but he quickly saw that they were strangers. In any case, if Ann were accompanying Graham, their two children, Richard and Susan, would also be with them. There were two empty seats on the aircraft, and the two new passengers took their places there. The aircraft was immediately prepared for takeoff, and within a few minutes they were airborne again. The aircraft turned as it climbed until it was flying north-west. There were more woods and fields, then suddenly they were flying over the Severn Estuary – grey-brown mudflats and silver water. On the far side, they passed a town on their left, but the green fields below soon gave way to hill country, with long, narrow valleys whose winding contours were marked out by terraces of miners' cottages with dark slate roofs. Beyond the valleys were the moors and high summits of the Brecon Beacons, green and grey. The aircraft began to encounter masses of cloud over the mountains, which were often obscured by the white mist. There was a break in the clouds as they crossed the coast, over the wide curve of Cardigan Bay. Looking down, Robert wondered when, if ever, he would set foot in the country again. At Croydon airport, just before they had left to go out to the aircraft, Robert had posted a letter to his boss at the Foreign Office, explaining why he had had to leave suddenly and without notice, and apologising for the necessity of doing so. It was the best he could do under the circumstances; but knowing his boss, Robert doubted whether it would be received with much sympathy. He had effectively burned his bridges.

After about forty minutes of cruising above the Irish Sea, the stewardess came forward to announce that the aircraft would shortly be landing. They had already started to lose height by the time they crossed the coast just south of the rounded expanse of Dublin Bay, which Robert could see through the window next to Mary. Mary, sitting on the right-hand side of the aircraft, had a good view of the centre of Dublin as they flew over, and was looking down with interest. Then they were landing, the wheels bumping over the grass of Baldonnel airfield. The aircraft turned as it taxied up to the hangars on the edge of the airfield, so that Robert had a view of them through his window. After the engines stopped, the stewardess opened the passenger door as the steps were put in place, and announced that passengers could now leave the aircraft.

"Can all those who wish to avail themselves of the bus transport into the city centre please stay together in a group with me," she said.

As he left the aircraft, Robert asked the stewardess if there would be time to make a couple of quick telephone calls before the bus left.

"Well, the bus leaves in about fifteen minutes, so if you're quick, there should be time," she told him.

The stewardess led the passengers past the hangars to the main airport building. The place looked very military and functional in comparison with Croydon. Inside the building, the stewardess pointed out the public telephones, and Robert went into one of the booths. The previous evening, he had spent some time looking through a recent AA handbook for Ireland, searching for hotels in Dublin. He had noticed that there were several two- and three-star hotels on Harcourt Street, apparently quite near each other. Having brought the handbook with him, he now opened it and started telephoning numbers. The first hotel he spoke to only had single rooms available, which was no good. With the second hotel, he had better luck. They had two double rooms free, which he booked immediately. The fourth hotel had a family room, which he booked for the Harveys. There was a tap at the window of the booth. It was Geoff Greenwood, who pointed at his watch, then over to where the rest of them were waiting. The bus was about to depart. Robert nodded, ended the phone call as quickly as he could, then hurried over to join the others with Geoff. He was only just in time. The others had been in something of a quandary, knowing that Robert was telephoning to book accommodation for them, but not wanting to get on the bus until they knew that he had been successful. Even as he hurried across, Robert waved to indicate that they should board the bus, which they proceeded to do. He rather breathlessly thanked the stewardess, who was standing by the entrance, and who looked meaningfully at her watch as he hurried past.

The bus was bound for the Aer Lingus office on Upper O'Connell Street, and passed through the centre of the city on its way there. It dropped them off on College Green, where some of the other passengers also alighted. From there they walked down Grafton Street, past St Stephen's Green, and on down to Harcourt Street. They reached the hotel Robert had booked for the Harveys first, which was a relief for the children, who by this time were tired and becoming fractious. The other hotel was about a hundred yards further on. After booking in, they found that they were still in time for the evening meal in the hotel's dining room.

Later, when they were in their room, Mary, who was sitting on the bed, looked at Robert.

"Are you sure we've done the right thing? What now?" she asked.

Robert sat down beside her.

"I've no doubt that we've done the right thing in leaving the country," he said. "I saw that list. It should be possible to confirm in the next day or two that Parliament has passed that Bill; and if it has, there's no doubt that I would have been arrested. As for the future, I'm expecting Mike Warren to arrive here in Dublin at the weekend. He has a house here, and he'll put us up there for the time being until we've found somewhere to live, and I've managed to find a job and an income. And by the weekend, we should have a clearer idea of what the situation is."

Three

The weekend brought developments that were both expected and unexpected. Most importantly, Mike Warren arrived in Dublin on the Saturday. One of the first things Robert had done on the Thursday morning, the day after they arrived in Dublin, was to send a postcard to Mike's London address. As did many hotels, the hotel they were staying at sold picture postcards with a view of the hotel on the front, with the address printed across at the bottom. On the back, Robert had scrawled: "Having a lovely time on holiday here in Ireland. John and Jane."

It was enough to let Mike know where they were. Robert suspected that all their mail was intercepted and read, but for delivery of mail to be stopped would be a new development. He could only hope for the best and see what happened.

Also on Thursday morning, Geoff and Sylvia walked to the Shelbourne Hotel on St Stephen's Green. When they enquired at the hotel's reception desk, they found that Elizabeth Lacey was indeed staying at the hotel. However, she had arrived very late the previous evening, and had left a 'do not disturb' instruction with hotel reception. They left a note for her, advising that they had arrived, and where they were staying. As they walked back, Sylvia remarked how Dublin seemed to be reminiscent of London in many ways. From Harcourt Street, they had walked across St Stephen's Green, as the Shelbourne Hotel was at the far corner of the green.

"Almost like an unfamiliar part of London," she said. It was the first time Sylvia had been to Dublin, or to Ireland.

On the Friday, by chance, Robert came across a job advert in the newspapers for a subeditor at *The Irish Times*. On an impulse he drafted a quick letter of application and posted it the same day. He didn't expect to get the job, but it would be interesting to see what response he got. It would 'test the waters' as far as the job market was concerned.

Also on the Friday, they finally met up with Elizabeth. Elizabeth Lacey was a widow, aged fifty-one. Her husband, John Lacey, had been a Major in the 7th Somerset Light Infantry, who was killed at the Third Battle of Ypres in August 1917. He was twenty-nine. He and Elizabeth had been married for five years, and had a four-year-old daughter, Jennifer. Elizabeth had been devastated by her husband's death, and had never recovered from it. He had been the love of her life, and she had never wanted to remarry. It was the main reason why she was staunchly opposed to another war in Europe, especially another war against Germany, and this had led her to join their group, National Renaissance. Her husband had been from a wealthy family, and she had been left well off as a widow. His family had connections in Ireland, and over the years Elizabeth had travelled to Ireland on a number of occasions, and she was fairly familiar with the country. In 1937 Jennifer had got married, and the following year, she and her husband had emigrated to Canada because of the lack of job opportunities in Britain following the Great Depression. Jennifer's departure had left quite a large gap in Elizabeth's life, and she had become more involved in National Renaissance as a result. It also meant that the idea of moving to Ireland to live now seemed more attractive. On the Friday evening, everyone met at the Shelbourne Hotel for dinner.

Much of Saturday was spent sightseeing around the centre of Dublin, when Elizabeth, who knew the city quite well, acted as their guide. On the Saturday evening there was a welcome visitor to the hotel where the Aldcrofts and Greenwoods were staying – Mike Warren. Mike's appearance was only brief, however. He had just arrived in Dublin, having flown from Croydon, and had only called in to announce his arrival. He was on his way to his house in Dublin, which, over the next two or three days, he would be getting ready for the rest of them to move into.

"I'll just be taking stock tomorrow," he said, "but I'll need your assistance from Monday morning onwards, so I'll look forward to seeing you then."

Mike Warren had stayed in the army after the end of the Great War, finally retiring at the age of forty, having come into a sizeable family inheritance, and was now of independent means. He had never married.

Sunday was spent quietly, with several of them, including Elizabeth, the Aldcrofts and the Greenwoods, attending the morning service at Christ Church Cathedral. There was still no news of war, beyond rumours of 'incidents' along the German-Polish frontier; although, as Robert knew, these had been going on for some time. He did find one item of interest in one of the British papers in the hotel lounge. In the Parliamentary Report, tucked away on an inside page, there was a brief mention of the Emergency Powers (Defence) Act, which had been passed that Thursday, the 24th. It gave no details about it, but Robert knew that this was the Act under which they were to have been interned. It confirmed that their flight to Dublin had not been in vain.

On the Monday morning, after breakfast, everyone assembled at the Harveys' hotel on Harcourt Street, and from there walked across to Camden Street, where they caught a bus down to Rathmines. They got off the bus outside Rathmines post office, and after consulting a map, set off for their destination. This was a large, detached house which Mike Warren had bought on Cambridge Road in Rathmines, a quiet, tree-lined residential street about five minutes' walk from the post office. Mike's house was near a bend in the road, about half-way down.

Within a few minutes of their arrival, Mike had organised them into two groups. Elizabeth, Mary and

Sylvia were despatched back to Rathmines high street with a list of provisions to buy or order, while the others were set to work removing dust sheets, moving furniture and cleaning, with the two children tagging along as interested observers. At the end of the day, much had been achieved. The house still wasn't ready, however, so the guests departed to their respective hotels. The following morning, everyone assembled as before and took the bus down to Rathmines. Mid-morning, the first two of the extra beds that had been ordered the previous day were delivered to the house in a furniture lorry, and by the end of the day, three bedrooms were ready. It was decided that everyone would move in the following day, Wednesday. The various hotels had been booked for seven nights, Tuesday being the last night.

On the Wednesday morning, after checking out of their hotels, everyone returned to the house. By lunchtime, the last of the beds and the two cots for the children had been delivered, and the last of the bedrooms made ready. That evening, Mike organised a celebratory dinner in honour of their arrival. It was very informal – they all sat around the heavy wooden table in the spacious kitchen at the back of the house. The atmosphere was relaxed, now that they had accomplished the move to Dublin.

"Well, the war didn't start at the weekend," Mike observed wryly to Robert.

Robert shook his head.

"All I can say is that at the Foreign Office last Wednesday, they were certain that the Germans would launch their attack on Poland on Saturday the 26th. Obviously I wasn't told what the source for that was, but I had the impression it was from somewhere inside Germany."

"Looks as if the source was wrong, then," said Mike.

"Well, obviously it was as far as the 26th is concerned. But even the Foreign Office only has a partial picture of what's going on. And situations change. The Anglo-Polish Treaty that was signed on Friday, the day before, might have had something to do with it. The text of the treaty was given in some of Saturday's papers."

"But that was just a restatement of the guarantee that Chamberlain gave to Poland back in March," said Geoff. "Surely that wouldn't change anything at this stage?"

"I wouldn't have thought so, no. And it doesn't seem to have changed the expectation that there's going to be a German attack."

"I think that expectation must be valid," said Mike. "Apart from anything else, troops can be kept in a state of readiness for attack only for so long. Eventually, the troops in the line have to be relieved and replaced by fresh troops, and once that starts happening, the initiative has been lost."

"And yet... and yet... we've been here before – with Czechoslovakia," said Geoff. "Few people doubted that Hitler fully intended to attack Czechoslovakia last September, even when the French said they would honour their treaty with the Czechs if he did."

"And it was Britain and France that backed down then, knowing that," said George. "Maybe another Munich Conference is being organised behind the scenes, and that's why the German attack didn't take place on Saturday."

"One can only hope so," said Geoff. "There have been reports in the press of an Italian peace initiative, and Bonnet is still in charge at the Quai d'Orsay, so if France and Italy can arrange a compromise, there might still be peace."

"The problem is Chamberlain," Robert observed. "He seems prepared recklessly to risk war with Germany over Poland, even though we cannot help Poland any more than we could have helped Czechoslovakia."

"Any objective observer would see it that way," agreed Geoff. "But Chamberlain seems to want war this time, and the Fleet Street press is shifting the mood of the country towards war."

"If the French are prepared to accept a settlement that gives Hitler what he wants, that would present Chamberlain with a *fait accompli,*" said George. "He surely wouldn't go to war with Germany without France. It looks as if everything depends on Bonnet and Mussolini now."

"I think that if anyone can pull something off, it will be Bonnet," agreed Christine. "He knows more than any French politician that the French people don't want to go through the Great War again, especially when France itself is not being attacked or threatened."

The others agreed.

"There is another aspect to that, though," Christine went on. "This Emergency Powers Act has now been passed by Parliament, so even if, by good fortune, war is avoided this time, that still leaves us as exiles here in Dublin."

"Unfortunately, that's true," said Robert. "The problem there is that as long as Chamberlain, or those of like mind are in power in London, war with Germany is always going to be imminent. Even if Chamberlain is thwarted this time by a Franco-Italian peace plan, he'll just wait for the next opportunity to go to war with Germany. As long as war is imminent in that way, they'll use this Emergency Powers Act against people like us."

"I would agree with that," said Mike. "It looks as if we're here for the long-term. And there's still no news about Graham."

Four

The following morning, Robert took the bus into the centre of Dublin and called in at the offices of *The Irish Times* on D'Olier Street. The previous day, just before they had checked out of the hotel, a letter had arrived for him. It was a response to his job application at *The Irish Times*, and it invited him to an interview on Friday 1st September. He decided to call in on the day before just to introduce himself.

When he explained why he had called in, he was told that the senior subeditor would not be in until that afternoon, given the paper's work schedule, but the senior staff manager was in and might see him if he would care to wait. Robert agreed and, after a short wait, the senior staff manager came through to the waiting room and introduced himself as Arthur Halloran.

"If you'd like to come through," Halloran said, and led Robert along to his office.

"We were intrigued by your letter," Halloran said, resuming the conversation. "Until last week you were a senior civil servant at the British Foreign Office. Now, you're applying for a job as a subeditor at *The Irish Times*. That's a rather extraordinary thing to do, to say the least."

Robert smiled wanly.

"As I'm sure you know, there's going to be a European war. If it doesn't start in the next few days over Poland, it'll be something else that will be used as a reason. The British Government are now determined to go to war with Germany. They've made a number of preparations." Robert explained briefly about the Emergency Powers Act. "Once I found out that my name was on the list of people to be arrested under the Act, I had to make arrangements to leave immediately. Dublin was the nearest safe place to go. Because the Act has now been passed, and looks like being in place for the foreseeable future, it means that I'm here for the long-term. Hence the job application."

"Yes, I remember we had a news item about that Act here in the *Times*," said Halloran. "Your departure from the Foreign Office must have been somewhat abrupt."

"It's not how I would have wanted it, but faced with being arrested and sent to prison without trial, presumably for many years, I didn't really have a lot of choice."

"This political association you belong to…"

"It's called National Renaissance. One of the things that has brought us together is opposition to another war with Germany. Since Chamberlain's Government have now decided to go to war with Germany, they've also decided that groups like ours are a danger to the state, and must be rounded up."

"Does that mean that you're pro-German – that you'd support Germany if there is a war?"

"No, it doesn't. I would never betray my country. What the Government can't accept is our belief that it would be a betrayal of the country to lead it into another war with Germany, another Great War, over an issue such as Czechoslovakia or Poland. Germany isn't threatening us, and there's nothing we can do to help Poland."

"But you can understand that such a view is not popular in Britain at the moment?"

"Of course. We've had to live with that for some time now. Although I should point out that it's not so long ago that the public mood was very different. I don't know if you remember the 1933 Fulham by-election, or the 1935 Peace Vote?"

"I do, but times have changed, obviously."

"They have, and the press has had a great deal to do with that. Even some of the left-wing press is now clamouring for war, so Chamberlain has the public behind him in his desire for war."

"I'm sure that's true. There's also an element of that here in Ireland. I don't know if you're aware that *The Irish Times* is generally pro-British in most respects. That goes back to well before the creation of the Free State, when the *Times* was part of the Unionist establishment."

"I think I was generally aware of that, yes. Would that have any bearing on my application to work for the *Times*?"

"It would be up to the senior subeditor to decide if it did. It might be thought odd for the *Times* to employ someone in your situation – a fugitive from British justice as some might see it. And given your views, some might ask why you would want to work for a newspaper that was generally pro-British."

"Well, I'm not anti-British. In fact, I regard myself as a patriot. It's not unpatriotic to disagree with the Government. And as far as justice is concerned, sending people to prison indefinitely without trial is hardly justice."

"I suppose I would have to agree with that. But they presumably have their reasons for reacting towards you in such a way."

"In my case, I think it's at least in part because of my position in the Foreign Office. I had access to a lot of information about what was going on behind the scenes, information not available to the ordinary man in the street. Given that the Government now regard me as politically undesirable, this is their response. As far as my job application is concerned, it might be of interest for you to have someone who has a lot of insight into how government works behind the scenes. I can't divulge specific information – as I said, I still regard myself as a patriot – but I can give you insights that most other people wouldn't have, whatever view you take of my politics."

"I'm sure that would be a point of interest. And if we only employed people who agreed with the editorial line on politics, we might struggle to staff the newspaper." He paused, then went on: "If there is war, what do you think will happen? Some are predicting that London would be flattened by a mass German bomber attack within twenty-four hours."

"That's certainly a view a lot of people take. There have been mass evacuations from the larger cities over the last few days, especially of children. We know that the Germans have at least 800 modern fast bombers capable of reaching London by crossing the North Sea from airfields in north-west Germany. If even half that number were used against London, the damage would be unimaginable."

"And yet Chamberlain seems prepared to take such a risk."

"On behalf of all those who will die. And then there will be another Western Front, with all that that means."

"Assuming that he can persuade the French to declare war as well."

"And that's looking doubtful. Georges Bonnet will do everything he can to stop France from being dragged into another war, especially over an issue such as Poland, and that's our main hope at the moment. Presumably even Chamberlain wouldn't be so stupid as to go to war against Germany without France."

"We'll presumably find out in the next couple of weeks or so," said Halloran. "Well, I'm glad you decided to call in. It's been an interesting conversation. I look forward to seeing you again tomorrow."

They shook hands.

From D'Olier Street, Robert made his way through the city centre towards Harcourt Street, to call in at the hotel they had stayed at to check if any mail had arrived for him since they left. His attention was caught by a flag on a building on the other side of the street he was walking along. The flag was bright red with a white disk in the centre, containing the now familiar inclined swastika. It was the German legation. Curious, he stopped for a minute to gaze at the building. Even as he watched, a car approached rapidly along the street and pulled up outside the legation in a squeal of brakes. A smaller version of the German flag fluttered from the front wing of the car. A young man with close-cropped blond hair, and carrying a briefcase, got out of the car and quickly ascended the steps to the door of the legation. The door opened as he did so, and he immediately went inside – he was evidently expected.

Something was obviously urgent.

Five

By eight-thirty on Friday morning, the smell of toast and fried bacon was wafting up from the kitchen to tempt the late risers down to breakfast. Some of the early risers had already finished breakfast. As this was only their second morning at the house, a definite routine had not yet been established. Mike, one of the early risers, had finished breakfast by this time and had gone through to the lounge to switch the wireless on. Not long afterwards he appeared in the kitchen with a concerned look on his face.

"There's just been a brief announcement on Irish Radio that the Germans are attacking Poland," he said. Everyone turned to look at him. "It didn't give any details. It said there would be more information in their scheduled news bulletin."

"I don't think that's until this evening," said Elizabeth. "It's an arrangement they have with the newspapers. Have you tried the BBC?"

"Yes, but they're not on the air yet. It looks as if they're keeping to their schedule, at least at the moment. There might be something when they start up at half-ten."

"What about continental stations?" Geoff asked.

"I haven't tried them. I'm not sure if Luxembourg will be on the air yet."

"Well, let's see."

He and Mike went back to the lounge, followed by Robert, Elizabeth and Sylvia. Mike tried Irish Radio again, to find it was in the middle of a schools programme. He then tried the BBC, but they were still not on the air. He turned the dial down until he found Berlin. At that moment, Berlin was playing martial music – Geoff recognised it as the overture to *Die Meistersinger*. After listening for a minute, Mike switched to long wave, and tuned to Luxembourg. Luxembourg was on the air, but was playing a programme of dance band music.

Noticing the name on the dial, Geoff pointed and said: "Try Warsaw."

Slowly, Mike turned the dial, searching for Warsaw. After a few moments, a man's voice emerged from the static. He was speaking continuously and rapidly, and even though none of them could understand the words, the note of urgency in his voice told its own story. After several minutes the man paused, during which there was the sound of papers being shuffled. When the man began speaking again, it was with the same rapid urgency as before. Whatever he was saying, it somehow didn't sound like an ordinary broadcast programme. Even as they listened, they heard a series of heavy explosions in the background of where the man was speaking from. The man paused for a few moments before saying something that might have been a comment on the sound of the explosions. He then continued to speak as before. As they continued to listen, he was again interrupted by the sound of explosions in the background.

"Sounds like it's true, then," said Mike. "I can tell that the heavier explosions are the sound of bombs, while the short, sharp explosions are the sound of guns – presumably anti-aircraft guns." Mike had served in the Royal Artillery on the Western Front. For Elizabeth, the sounds brought back memories of the German bombing of London during the Great War.

"If they're bombing Warsaw, it must be more than just an operation to seize Danzig and the Corridor," observed Geoff.

"You may well be right," said Mike, "although they might bomb Warsaw and other places as a diversionary tactic. We'll probably have to wait for more news to confirm that it's a general assault."

Robert didn't have time to wait any longer, however, if he was to keep the appointment for his interview at *The Irish Times*. A few minutes later he left the house to catch a bus into the city centre. At D'Olier Street, he was taken upstairs to a waiting room next to where the interviews were taking place. When he was called through, he found there were just two people on the interview board – Arthur Halloran, and the senior subeditor, who was introduced by Halloran as James Doyle.

After some routine questions, Robert was given a test to complete. He had to condense a sports report into no more than 200 words, in no more than ten minutes. It was a report about a football match and, although he wasn't particularly familiar with football, he completed the task within the ten minutes allowed.

After reading through it, Doyle commented: "Not bad. Have you done this before?"

"Not for a newspaper; but at the Foreign Office I often had to write reports, and also write précis of reports and documents written by others, so I'm familiar with the general idea."

"Yes, Arthur mentioned the conversation you had yesterday. You're rather an unusual character; although I have heard that a number of people from across the water have come to Dublin because of the war, including the author T. H. White."

"I hadn't heard about T. H. White, but I can well believe it. But as Mr Halloran will have told you, in my case it was because I was presented with a rather stark choice of fleeing or ending up in prison. There may not be many of us who are opposed to war, but the prospect of war is not universally popular, even in Britain."

"But if there is war, life won't be easy for those who oppose it. You certainly seem to be in an unusual situation yourself. Have you heard the news this morning?"

"About the German attack on Poland? Yes, I have." Robert described how they had listened in to Radio Warsaw earlier that morning. He could tell that they were both interested and impressed by his account, and by the end of the interview, he felt quite pleased with his performance. As he walked back towards College

Green from D'Olier Street, he went over the interview in his mind, and decided it had been a very worthwhile experience, even if he didn't get the job. It had been a long time since he had last sat for an external job interview.

On College Green, there was a news vendor with the early edition of one of the evening papers. Robert bought one, and saw that it was a special edition, with the first reports of the attack on Poland. The reports seemed to confirm that it was a general attack at many points along the Polish border, and not just at Danzig and the Corridor. It was reported that many places had been bombed by German aircraft, including Warsaw.

By this time, the pubs had opened, so he had some lunch at the Stag's Head on Dame Court. He read through the paper while eating lunch; but apart from the reports on the front page, there was no further news about the war. It was essentially a 'stop press' edition. From the snatches of conversation he could hear around him, the news about Poland hadn't yet impinged much on the lives of average Dubliners. Everyone knew about the impending war; but the general expectation was that Ireland would stay neutral in the event of war, so the perspective here was very different from the one in London. Politics in Ireland was almost completely dominated by recent events and, in particular, by the political divisions created by the civil war. Events outside Ireland tended to be seen through the lens of Irish politics, and were refracted by its divisions.

That evening, at Mike's house on Cambridge Road, they all listened to the announcements about the German attack, on both Irish radio and the BBC. The reports confirmed that the German attack was a general assault on the whole of Poland. There was no news of the response of the British and French Governments; but the BBC reported that there would be a sitting of Parliament on the morrow at which the prime minister, Mr Chamberlain, would make a statement. Irish radio reported that the Irish Parliament, the Dail, would be recalled for an emergency session on the morrow because of the German attack.

"It looks," observed Mike, "as if we're in for an interesting weekend."

Six

Mike was proved right. Saturday was a day of uncertainty. The morning news bulletin on the BBC, after reporting that the German attack on Poland was continuing, gave the text of the British communique which had been sent to the German Government the previous evening, warning the Germans that Britain would honour its commitment to Poland if they didn't cease their attack and withdraw. A similar warning had been issued by the French Government. There was no indication of any response from the Germans. A bit later on, Sylvia, who spoke French, listened in to French radio from Paris. She said that there were reports on French radio that the French foreign minister, Georges Bonnet, was seeking Italian support for a conference of the four powers who were at Munich, to try and arrange a ceasefire and a settlement that would prevent the conflict from becoming a European war.

"It looks as if Georges Bonnet will be Europe's last hope for peace," said Christine when she heard this.

"I'm sure you're right," said Mike, "although I'm not sure if the present situation isn't now beyond even Bonnet. I think a lot now depends on the attitude of the French General Staff. I suspect that many of them are deeply reluctant to face another war with Germany."

Later that day, another cause for concern arose, with reports on Irish radio about the Emergency Powers Act that De Valera's Government was rushing through the Irish Parliament as a response to the outbreak of war. Of particular concern were reports that the Act would contain powers of detention without trial, which sounded ominously similar to the ones in the British Act.

"I hope this doesn't mean that we've jumped out of the frying pan and into the fire," Mary commented after they had listened to the last news bulletin of the day on Irish radio.

"Perhaps those of us who aren't on the arrest list in London should return to Britain if that's the case," said Robert. "You came here only because of us," he went on, turning to Mary as he did so.

But Mike was shaking his head.

"I doubt very much whether this has anything to do with people like us. If I'm not mistaken, it's because the Irish Government, even De Valera's Government, regards the IRA as a continuing serious threat to its security."

"I would agree with that," said Elizabeth. "I'm fairly sure that this has everything to do with the IRA, bearing in mind recent events here in Ireland. I'd be inclined to see this in the context of Irish politics."

"Well, you both know this country better than the rest of us, so I trust you're right about that," said Robert.

"I'm fairly confident about it, from what I know of Irish politics over the last few years. If the Irish Government does have an arrest list – which I suspect it will do – then everyone on it will almost certainly be members or associates of the IRA. The IRA are determined to continue the Civil War, even now that De Valera's in office, and from what I've heard just now," Mike indicated the wireless, "it sounds as if De Valera intends to crush them."

"Sounds a bit like what Hitler did to the Brownshirts in 1934," observed Geoff.

"That's probably quite a good analogy," said Mike. "The last thing the Government wants at this point is a resumption of the Civil War, so it looks as if it's not taking any chances."

"It should become clear enough in the next few days," said Elizabeth.

The following morning, they heard an announcement on the BBC that the prime minister was to make a statement, which would be broadcast shortly after eleven o'clock. The early news bulletins that morning reported that the German attack on Poland was continuing. Just before 11.15am there was an announcement of the statement by the prime minister. After a pause of a few moments, Chamberlain's voice sounded from the speaker. They all listened to the statement in silence. When it was finished, everyone was silent for a few moments longer.

Elizabeth then said: "His conscience is clear? Well, lucky for him!"

"I wonder if his conscience will still be clear at the end of this business, whatever that turns out to be," said Geoff.

An hour or so later, Sylvia, listening to Paris, said that there had been an announcement on French radio that France had delivered a similar ultimatum to the Germans, which would expire at 5pm French time.

Later that afternoon, Robert and Mary went for a walk to see something of the area in which they were now living. Rathmines was a prosperous suburb of south Dublin, with tree-lined roads and large semi-detached or detached houses with gardens and driveways. It might have been one of the more well-to-do areas of north London. It was pleasant walking in the late summer sunshine, and not far away they found a park in the centre of a square called Belgrave Square. Children were playing football there, and quite a few other people were, like them, out for a Sunday afternoon stroll. There was no war here, and everything was normal. In this place, one might easily imagine that the war was a fantasy that would pass like a bad dream in the face of this seemingly solid reality.

Mary squeezed Robert's hand.

"We did the right thing coming here," she said. "It would be unthinkable to be in London now, with what must be going on there."

"What price sanity? But it's a price we've had to pay."

A short distance away they came across the Leinster Cricket Club. There was a cricket match in progress, and for a while they stood and watched from the road that ran alongside the cricket ground. As they watched, the batsman was caught and bowled, and slowly made his way back to the pavilion to a smattering of applause from a small group of spectators standing along the edge of the field. He waved his bat in acknowledgment. The fielders regrouped, waiting for the next batsman in. To Mary, as she watched, it seemed hard to believe that they were not somewhere in England.

Back on Cambridge Road, they went to have a look at the church at the southern end of the road, which turned out to be a church of the Anglican communion – Holy Trinity, Church of Ireland. They were too late for the services that day, but the church was still open, and they went inside to have a look. There was no-one else in the church, and after walking round, they sat down together in one of the pews at the front of the nave. The interior was plain and subdued, with white painted walls, and with little stained glass in the windows. The afternoon sunlight streamed through the windows of the nave behind them, throwing pools of light across the rows of pews and the walls opposite. The hymn board still contained the hymn numbers for the last service. Dust motes floated lazily in the streams of light. The stillness was complete. Mary closed her eyes and offered up a short prayer.

"On this day, of all days…"

***

The evening news bulletins confirmed that the French ultimatum had expired without a response, and that France was also at war with Germany.

"Well, Chamberlain has got his war," observed Mike, "however much he professes not to have wanted one."

"Everything he worked for is now in ruins," said Elizabeth, with sarcasm. "Well, he could have resigned if he didn't want to be seen as being responsible for the war; but he hasn't."

"I think his responsibility for the war goes back at least to the guarantee given to Poland in March," said Geoff. "I don't think he could avoid it by resigning now."

"As with most politicians, I think he should be judged by his actions rather than his words," said Robert.

"And yet, most people in England now would protest that there was no other course of action he could have taken," observed Christine.

"That might be the case now, if he isn't prepared to resign," said Mike. "But as we all know, and as Geoff said just now, Chamberlain's responsibility for the war goes back at least as far as the guarantee to Poland in March, if not to Munich, or earlier."

"The Peace Vote of '35 seems like another era now," Christine mused.

"Public opinion is all too easily manipulated," said George. "People are influenced by what they're told – and, perhaps more importantly, by what they're not told."

"Perhaps there's something we might do in that regard," said Mike.

"How do you mean?" asked Robert.

"Well, if the history of these events is written by those who are in power at the moment, then their view of the situation will become the historical orthodoxy.

Inconvenient facts and circumstances will be written out of the history. As George said just now, it's often what people are not told that's most significant in forming their view of events. The idea occurs to me that we here could form a kind of committee of inquiry to look into all the factors that have led to this war, not least being Chamberlain's role in it, and then set down our findings to set against the official histories that will be written by those who are responsible for the war. Even if we're only a small voice crying in the wilderness, I think it's something that needs to be done by someone. In some ways, we're well-placed to carry out such an inquiry here in Dublin, outside the immediate turmoil of the war."

"That could prove to be quite a major task, even for a group of us," said Geoff, smiling wryly.

"Assuming that nothing untoward happens on this side of the Irish Sea, we should have the time and the opportunity. And we have the National Library of Ireland, one of the best libraries in Europe, just down the road."

"I think it's an excellent idea," said Elizabeth. "In fact, I think, given the situation we're in, we have a moral responsibility to carry out such an inquiry. I can't think of anyone else who's likely to do so."

Everyone else agreed. After further discussion it was decided to hold the first formal meeting of the committee the following morning.

Seven

The following day, after breakfast, everyone assembled in the drawing room. Mike had set the room up for the meeting, bringing in extra chairs so that everyone had a seat around the main table. At every seat he had placed a sheet of paper and a pencil. The two children were settled in a corner of the room with colouring books to occupy them.

After everyone had taken their seats, Mike declared the committee to be in session. The first item on the agenda was what the committee should be called. After some debate, it was decided to call it The Independent Committee of Inquiry into Responsibility for the War between Great Britain and Germany. For the time being, Mike acted as secretary, mainly because he had a large notebook in which to record the committee's proceedings.

Geoff opened the discussion. As a professional writer and historian, he had a considerable fund of knowledge about the background to the situation they were now discussing.

"Focusing on the war itself," he said, "Britain has declared war on Germany because Germany has attacked Poland. This focuses attention on two principal questions, which could form the basis of the whole inquiry: why Germany, rather than, say, Italy, or any other country? And why over Poland, rather than Czechoslovakia, or any of the other recent disputes in Europe? These are obviously very broad questions, and the answers to them will involve many different factors: history, geography, political considerations, military and strategic considerations, economic and industrial considerations, to name but some of them. I suggest that we should first of all map out all the areas of investigation which we agree are relevant to the inquiry. We can then allocate these to one or other of us to carry out the detailed investigation into each area. Demonstrating responsibility doesn't just mean demonstrating a link to a chain of events. It also means demonstrating how alternative courses of action could have been taken – most obviously, that of not seeking confrontation with Germany to a point which has now led to war. It's a major task, which will keep all of us more than fully occupied – in fact, we might even need to call on the assistance of the children before we're finished," he said with a smile, looking over to where the two children, oblivious of this, were absorbed with their colouring books.

***

During the rest of that week they agreed the detailed areas of investigation that needed to be carried out, and also who would be responsible for each of the areas of investigation. Even by the end of that week, it was clear that the war was going badly for Poland. On Wednesday 6th September, the Germans captured Cracow, and by the Friday, German forces had reached the outskirts of Warsaw, and the Polish Government had had to leave the capital. Mike began to keep a chronicle of events in the progress of the war, and on the Wednesday a large wall map of Europe was purchased from a bookshop in Dublin and was put up in the drawing room. A file for newspaper clippings with articles about the war was also created.

One surprise on the Friday was the arrival of a letter for Robert from *The Irish Times*, offering him a job as a subeditor, starting on Monday 18th September. Robert immediately wrote back accepting the offer. It would mean that he wouldn't have as much time as the others to devote to the Committee of Inquiry, but he would be contributing financially to the household, which for him was the most important thing.

By this time it was becoming a matter of concern that nothing had been heard from Graham Shepherd. The personal column of *The Irish Times* was being checked every day, but there had been nothing there either from Graham or Duncan. As Graham's name had been on the list of people to be arrested under the Emergency Powers Act, if he was still in England, he would now undoubtedly be in grave danger. On the Saturday morning, 9th September, a discussion was held about what should be done.

"Surely," said George, "if Graham knew his name was on that list, he wouldn't risk staying in England?"

"He would be faced with a choice between leaving his family or trying to bring them out with him," observed Elizabeth. "Perhaps it proved too difficult to bring his family out, given that they live in a remote location in Essex."

"Perhaps they're still trying to get out," suggested Sylvia.

"If they're still anywhere in England, that won't be easy now," said Mike. "Especially if it's the whole family. In fact, it will now be extremely risky to try using regular ports or airports if his name is on that list and they're looking for him."

"If there was some way of contacting him, or at least trying to find out what's happened…" said Sylvia.

"Do you think it would be justifiable to risk trying to contact him by telephone?" Mary asked.

"I think it would," said Mike, "and I've an idea about how that might be done." He turned to Robert. "Bob, do you have that AA handbook for Ireland handy?"

Robert went to fetch it.

Mike perused the handbook for a few minutes, turning to the map pages before giving a nod of satisfaction.

"Right, this is what I propose to do. On Monday, I'll take the train up to Dundalk, which is just south of the border with Northern Ireland, for those not familiar with the geography here. I'll take my bicycle along, and from Dundalk I'll cycle to this place here – a village called Forkhill – which is just over the border in Northern

Ireland. According to the handbook, there's a public telephone box in Forkhill, so I'll make the telephone call from there. That'll have two advantages. Firstly, as it will be from within the United Kingdom, it won't be flagged up at the exchange as being a foreign call, which it would be if I called from here or anywhere in the Free State. Secondly, it'll improve my chances of actually getting through when I make the call. The telephone system here in the Free State hasn't been changed since before the war – the Great War, I mean – and it's now hopelessly antiquated."

"That would be risky," observed Robert.

"I think the risk will be fairly low," said Mike. "Even if they're doing border checks on trains crossing the border – and I haven't heard that they're doing even that – there's no way that they could do border checks on the hundreds of little roads that cross the border in remote rural areas like this. It would be totally impracticable. And even if the exchange registered that a call had been made to Graham's number and alerted the authorities, by the time they were able to get someone to that location – probably a policeman on a bicycle – I would be long gone. Forkhill is only just over the border. Along this side road here," – he pointed to the map – "the border is only a few hundred yards away."

"Do you want someone to come with you?" asked Geoff. "I'm game if you do."

"Thanks Geoff, but I think it's best if I do this on my own. Two cyclists together are a lot more conspicuous than one cyclist on his own. And even if the risk is small, there's no point in more than one of us taking it."

"Well, as long as you're sure…"

"I'm sure it will be an interesting day out," said Mike with a smile.

Mike's expectations proved to be correct. On the Monday morning, he set out on his bicycle and cycled into Dublin, to Amiens Street station, to catch a morning train to Dundalk. The others watched him set off with some concern. A little later, Geoff, Elizabeth, Robert and Mary made their way to the National Library of Ireland on Kildare Street to undertake research for the Committee of Inquiry. As they were each pursuing their own lines of research, they each made their own way back to Mike's house on Cambridge Road during the late afternoon. They were all back by six o'clock, and an evening meal was prepared, but there was still no sign of Mike. By eight o'clock, when the evening meal was over, there was growing concern that Mike had still not returned.

"If Mike doesn't turn up tonight, I think one or two of us should go to this place Forkhill and ask around to find out if anyone saw what happened," said Sylvia. "I'd be prepared to do that."

"We need to think carefully before doing that," said Geoff. "Remember, Mike's name wasn't on the list, so if they've arrested him, they could arrest any of us."

"One thing we should do if he hasn't turned up by morning is to notify the Irish police that Mike has gone missing, and explain the circumstances," said Robert. "If Mike's been arrested under the Emergency Powers Act, that will almost certainly mean that he'll just disappear without trace. There will be no judicial proceedings – no trial. He'll just be bundled into a prison cell somewhere. The suspension of *Habeas Corpus* means that people can just disappear if that suits the authorities. The Irish police will be better placed than any of us to demand answers and explanations from the British authorities."

"I wish we'd tried more to persuade him not to go," said Christine. "Even if it would be more difficult to try phoning from here…"

However, at that moment, they heard a sound at the back door, and a minute later Mike was standing in the kitchen doorway. For a moment, they all looked startled. Mike, seeing the empty dishes still on the table, said: "I hope you've saved me some tea – I'm starving!"

Elizabeth, smiling, said: "I'm afraid we haven't, Mike. But it won't take a minute to rustle up something. You'll have to sing for your supper, though. We're all waiting to hear what you've been up to."

***

Mike settled back in his chair after finishing his supper and yawned mightily before beginning his tale.

"Well," he said, "ever since deciding to make this trip I'd been turning over in my mind the question of when would be the best time to make the telephone call. Eventually I decided that the best time would be early evening, because most people are at home at that time, even if they've been out during the day, or are planning to go out again in the evening. I finally settled on this time while I was on the train going up to Dundalk. This meant that I was going to have rather a lot of time on my hands before I could actually make the call. So, on arriving in Dundalk, I first of all cycled from the station into the town centre to have a look around. Dundalk is just a market town, fairly undistinguished, apart from its Roman Catholic cathedral, which is quite a remarkable building for an otherwise nondescript place.

"After noting one or two likely-looking pubs in the town centre, I decided to do a preliminary recce of the job first, and set off along the road north out of the town. Forkhill is about five miles north of Dundalk, and it's a fairly straight road all the way, so it took me about half an hour to get there going at a fairly moderate pace. Forkhill is a long straggly village, so I had to cycle the best part of a mile before I reached what I took to be the centre of it."

"Were there any checks at the border?" asked George.

"Nothing at all," said Mike. "The only indication that the border was there at all was a small flat stone set into the roadside verge that said 'County Armagh' on one side of it, and 'County Louth' on the other. That was it. There was no-one around that I could see. I was alone on the road. It was open countryside all around.

"So, having reached Forkhill and noted the location of the telephone box, I left the village along the side road I mentioned before. This cuts across to another road running north from Dundalk, but along this side road the border is much closer, and I was back in County Louth within a few minutes. Half an hour later I was back in Dundalk, and I decided to have a late lunch at one of the pubs in the town centre which I'd noted earlier. During the late afternoon I went into the local library to look at some maps of the area, and in the early evening I set off again along the road up to Forkhill. Again, there were no problems. From the telephone box, I had to ask the local operator to put the call through, which she did. After a minute or so, she came back on the line to say that there was no reply from Graham's number. I thanked her and ended the call. After thinking about it for a couple of minutes, I decided that I would try again later. There's a pub just down the road from the telephone box, so I went in there to have a drink. From a seat by one of the front windows I could see the telephone box, and kept it under observation for the next hour. No-one went into it during that time, and there was no sign of the police. After finishing my drink, I went back to the telephone box and tried again. It was the same as before. After a minute or so, the operator came back on the line to say that there was no reply from that number. There was nothing more I could do at that point, so I cycled back to Dundalk the same way as before, and caught the next train back to Dublin."

"I think you have done very well," said Elizabeth warmly.

"Indeed," Robert concurred. "Do you think it means that Graham must have left the house?"

"It looks that way," said Mike. "Not to be at home on a Monday evening is generally fairly unusual unless one is away from home. However, if we haven't heard anything from Graham before much longer, we'll need to make a decision about what else we can do."

Eight

By the second weekend of the war, it was beginning to look, even from the news reports, as if Poland's fate had already been sealed. By the 9th of September, German forces had overrun most of western Poland and reached the line of the Vistula and San rivers from just south of Warsaw all the way down to Przemysl near the southern border. The Germans crossed the Polish Corridor on 5th September. Cracow fell on the 6th September, Tarnow on the 7th, and Lodz on the 8th. On the 8th, German forces reached the western outskirts of Warsaw, and the Polish Government had evacuated to Lublin. Lublin in turn fell on the 11th September, and the Polish Government and remaining Polish forces were reported to be retreating towards the Romanian border to make a last stand, although there were also reports of a Polish counter-attack west of Warsaw. Radio Warsaw remained on the air, as they confirmed by listening in most days, and although none of them could understand what was being broadcast, it seemed to confirm that resistance was continuing in Warsaw, albeit under increasingly desperate conditions, to judge by the tone of the broadcasts, and the sound of explosions, presumably German bombs, in the background.

The Committee of Inquiry's routine was becoming well established by this time. They had divided themselves into three teams. Mike was the Committee secretary, and his team, which included Elizabeth, George and Christine, was documenting the progress of the war and associated political events, mostly from newspaper reports, but also from the news bulletins on the BBC and Irish radio. A large ledger book was purchased, into which news reports were written and newspaper cuttings were pasted. George and Christine were also occupied with looking after the children and, for the time being at least, attending to their education. Christine decided to involve the children in creating a ledger documenting how the war was affecting children, to give them a sense of being part of the project. Robert and Mary were responsible for researching the political, economic and military background to the war, and Geoff and Sylvia were responsible for researching the historical background. As there would inevitably be quite a lot of overlap between these areas, regular conferences were held to coordinate the information that was to be recorded.

On Sunday, 17th September, Robert was making preparations for starting work at *The Irish Times* the following morning. He had called in to the newspaper's offices on the Friday, to confirm any last-minute requirements. However, the Sunday routine, which by now included attendance at the morning service at Holy Trinity Church at the end of Cambridge Road, was electrified by the evening news bulletin on the BBC, with a report that Soviet forces had invaded Poland, all along its eastern border. According to the BBC, it was a large-scale invasion, rather than just a border incursion, and had begun early that morning. At that point, there wasn't much more information than that. There was no doubt, however, even from these early reports, that this was a momentous event.

The following day, Monday, proved to be an interesting one for Robert. On arrival at *The Irish Times*, after being greeted by Arthur Halloran, the senior staff manager, and completing the formalities of being taken on as a new employee, he was conducted, mid-morning, to the subeditors' office. Somewhat to his disappointment, the senior subeditor, James Doyle, allocated him for the time being to the sports desk, rather than the main news desk. However, all the subeditors shared one large office, so whenever he had a few minutes to spare, Robert could drift over to the main news desk to see what news stories were coming through. At the end of that day, Robert returned to Cambridge Road feeling pleased with the first day of his new job. Little further news about Poland had come through during the day, and nor was there much more information about the Soviet invasion on the BBC's evening news bulletin, although there was a report that the Polish Government, led by President Moscicki, had crossed into Romania.

"There doesn't seem to be much talk of Britain declaring war on Soviet Russia," commented Mike on the Tuesday.

"So much for the moral high ground and treaty obligations," Geoff observed. "If there isn't a declaration of war against Soviet Russia, I think that will be a significant piece of evidence for our enquiry."

The others agreed. But the days passed, and there was no sign of any such declaration of war. The Soviet invasion forestalled any possibility of a Polish national redoubt on the Romanian frontier, and the end for Poland soon followed. On the 22nd of September, Lwow was occupied by Soviet forces, and Warsaw capitulated on the 27th, being occupied by the Germans on 1st October. In Mike's house on Cambridge Road, they heard the last transmission of Radio Warsaw before it closed down as the Germans moved in. The last Polish forces still resisting surrendered on 6th October. And that was it. By this time the Polish Government had re-formed in exile in Paris; but Poland had effectively ceased to exist, having been partitioned between the Germans and the Soviets.

***

After a month in his new job at *The Irish Times*, Robert felt that he had settled in well. The routine of the job was much more mundane than his work at the Foreign Office had been, but it was not without interest, and being close to the news desk meant that he was in a position to see the news as it was coming in. Robert's commitment to his job meant that he now had much less time than the others to devote to research for the Committee of Inquiry. George had approached a number of accountancy firms in Dublin, and had been taken on as an assistant accountant on a part-time basis by one of them. This meant that he too now had much less time to devote to the Committee, but his fees provided useful extra income for the household. These developments necessitated some changes in the workload of the Committee, with Mary now taking on most of the research work in her area, with additional help from Geoff when required.

Geoff had attempted to re-establish contact with his publisher in London, using the General Post Office in Dublin as a *poste restante* address. Eventually he received a reply from the publisher. The letter informed him that the company would have nothing to do with traitors and had terminated his contract; and also that Geoff's letters to them had been passed to the police. Geoff showed the letter to the others.

"Did you tell them that you were leaving the country?" asked Robert. "I posted a letter to my boss just before we boarded the aeroplane at Croydon."

Geoff shook his head.

"It's not like a day job, where you have to account for yourself every day. I'm only in contact with them intermittently, when I submit something for publication, or they contact me about something I've submitted. The first time I advised them that I was in Ireland was in the first letter I sent to them from the General Post Office here in Dublin. But even in that letter, I didn't say anything about why I had come to Ireland. I suspect that what happened was that after the police went to our home in London and found us gone, they then must have gone to my publisher. What exactly the police told them I don't know, but judging by this letter, it's not hard to guess."

"It's further confirmation, if any were needed, of how accurate your warning was," George said to Robert. Robert nodded in reply.

"Could you sue them for breach of contract?" asked Christine.

Geoff shrugged.

"There was no need for them to have mentioned it at all. They could simply have declined anything I sent them as being 'unsuitable', or something along those lines. If they've terminated my contract, that tells a story in itself. As for suing them, not this side of the war, that's for sure. If I had to give testimony to the court in person, that would rule it out straight away. And even if it got to court, regardless of the merits of the case, I can't see any court in Britain ruling in my favour now. They say that the first casualty of war is the truth. That's closely followed by justice. It looks as if everyone over there from the top down has enthusiastically followed Mr Chamberlain into his war. They aren't going to let a little matter like justice stand in their way."

Again, Robert nodded in agreement, and then said:

"But having thus made their bed, I suspect that they'll find, before very much longer, that they'll have to lie on it."

Nine

In early December, at a general meeting of the Committee, it was decided that their research had reached a point where they were in a position to produce a preliminary report of their findings and that it was now desirable to do so. The long-term outlook was now discouraging, and it was felt necessary to set down their findings about the causes of the war, before the impending escalation of the war overshadowed the circumstances of its origin. On 6th October, Hitler had made a speech to the Reichstag, which was widely publicised, in which he had proposed a peace conference to end the war before the fighting began in earnest. Six days later, on 12th October, Chamberlain, addressing the House of Commons, unequivocally rejected Hitler's proposal. As they listened to that evening's BBC news bulletin on the wireless in Mike's house, it seemed clearer than ever to all of them that Chamberlain was determined to have an all-out war with Germany. The issue was no longer about Poland. Poland had ceased to exist. The issue was about war with Germany. What Chamberlain wanted was a return to the Great War.

By the beginning of December, much work had been achieved by the Committee after nearly three months of fairly intensive research, particularly into the historical background to the war. Although much work remained to be done, and the work would inevitably continue at least for the duration of the war, since the course of the war itself would also form part of the Committee's evidence, by early December, it was felt that enough work had already been done to allow an interim presentation of evidence to be made. With the war in Poland over, but with no major fighting in the West, it was as if events were suspended in the balance, and it was a moment for reflection.

A couple of days were needed to assemble the material they had for presentation. The first part of the interim presentation was by Geoff and Sylvia, about the historical background to the war.

"Since the justification for this war is the German attack on Poland, it means that one focus of this inquiry should be the historical background to the conflict between Germany and Poland," said Geoff, leading off the presentation.

"It's a background that goes back a long way. At the time of the Roman Empire, Germanic peoples inhabited most of the north European plain, from what is now the Netherlands in the west," he turned and pointed at the wall map of Europe, which was set up behind him, "to the river Vistula in the east, in what is now Poland, and also southern Scandinavia. The Germanic people were one of the main sub-divisions of the Indo-European people who invaded and conquered Europe during the Bronze Age, before 1000 BC. This conquest took the form of a series of invasions by different Indo-European tribes over a period of several centuries. Among the earliest Indo European invaders were the Greeks, the Celts – who established an Iron Age civilisation right across Central Europe – the Germanic people, who settled most of north-west Europe, and the Italic peoples, who settled in Italy. The Slavic people didn't arrive until much later, towards the end of the Roman Empire. The end of the Roman Empire was a time of mass migration of people in Europe, with a general movement westward. One of the main causes of the downfall of the Roman Empire was large-scale invasions by Germanic tribes, who seized sizeable parts of it. This migration of the Germanic people left parts of their original homeland, particularly in the east, largely depopulated. These territories, particularly between the Vistula and the Elbe, saw a major influx of Slavic people during the fifth to seventh centuries AD. By the eighth century AD, the most powerful of the German tribes, the Franks, had established a kingdom which encompassed most of what is now France and most of Germany west of the Elbe. Its most famous ruler was Charlemagne, who had himself crowned Holy Roman Emperor in 800 AD. After Charlemagne's death, however, the Frankish kingdom split, eventually into the Kingdom of the West

Franks, and the Kingdom of the East Franks. The western kingdom became France. The name Holy Roman Empire eventually attached only to the eastern kingdom, and it was this which was the origin of modern Germany."

"So the original inhabitants of the area where the present war is being fought were German," said Christine.

"Yes, certainly going back to the earliest historical records, mainly by Greek and Roman historians," replied Geoff. "And in fact, when those historians were writing, Germanic tribes had probably already been settled there for several centuries. The Slavic people didn't start arriving in this area until much later, from about the fifth century AD onwards."

"So when does Poland as a country date from?" asked George.

"Well, the early history of the Slavic people is obscure, because prior to the arrival of Christian missionaries and the introduction of Christianity there was no literacy, and therefore no written records. Records of the Slavs from other sources, mainly the Byzantines, don't give a lot of detail. The original homeland of the Slavic tribes seems to have been an area in what is now Ukraine and western Russia, to the north of the Black Sea." He turned to the map and pointed.

"In the fifth and sixth centuries AD there was a major migration of Slavs westward into Central Europe, and south-westward into the Balkans. Following these migrations, the Slavs began to differentiate into the tribes that would eventually form the bases of modern Slavic nations. The Poles as an ethnic group seem to have emerged by about the tenth century AD. Traditionally, Poland dates its foundation from 966 AD, when its first ruler, Mieszko I, was baptised a Christian. Poland at that time seems to have extended as far west as the river Oder, including the Baltic coast between the Oder and the Vistula rivers. The land between the Oder and the Elbe was largely inhabited by tribes such as the Wends, who, although Slavic, were independent of Poland.

"By the tenth century, however, the Germans of the Holy Roman Empire were starting to push eastward from the Elbe, to reclaim some of their ancestral homeland from the Slavs. By 962, when Otto the Great was crowned Holy Roman Emperor, the boundaries of the Empire had been pushed eastwards as far as the river Oder. It was an uncertain process at first, as there was considerable resistance from the Slavic tribes, but by 1100 AD, the land west of the Oder had been fully incorporated into the Empire, and the process of Germanisation was begun. This brought the Empire into direct contact with the Kingdom of Poland, and the long struggle between the two dates from this time. During the twelfth and thirteenth centuries, the struggle was mainly over control of Pomerania." He indicated the area on the map. "Pomerania was a semi-independent country, initially populated by Slavic tribes. During the twelfth century, the Empire consolidated its hold on Western Pomerania, albeit with occasional reverses, and it was Germanised by settlement. By the end of the fourteenth century, Eastern Pomerania and Silesia had been incorporated into the Empire, followed by the process of Germanisation by settlement. It was a slow process, often complicated by reverses, and also interventions by other powers, particularly Denmark, which also had territorial designs on Pomerania.

"Then in 1230, the Teutonic Order, which had been founded in 1190 during the Third Crusade to the Holy Land, launched the Prussian Crusade, to conquer and Christianise the Baltic Prussians." He turned and pointed to the map.

"You mean East Prussia?" asked George.

"Well, strictly speaking, no. It's a point of confusion, so I'll need to explain. The Prussian Crusade of 1230 was launched against the Old Prussians, sometimes also called the Baltic Prussians. The Old Prussians were not Germans, but Balts. The Balts are a separate Indo-European people with their own distinct language group, which includes Latvian and Lithuanian, as well as languages which have now died out, such as Old Prussian. Very little is known about the early history of the Balts, as they converted to Christianity only towards the end of the Middle Ages, and had no written history before that time; but it's assumed that the Balts arrived in their present location, around the south-eastern corner of the Baltic, during the same period when the other Indo-European peoples were moving into Europe. In the thirteenth century, they were still pagans. The pagan Old Prussians had become a serious menace to the Polish kingdom, to the extent that the King of Poland eventually requested the assistance of the Teutonic Order to deal with them. However, in doing so, the Poles merely exchanged one problem for another. After a long campaign lasting several decades, the Knights of the Teutonic Order finally crushed the Old Prussians and occupied their territory, which was roughly the same as that of modern East Prussia. However, having done so, the Teutonic Knights then turned their attention to Poland itself. They annexed the land around the cities of Kulm and Thorn in northern Poland, which the Poles had leased to them as a base from which to launch their crusade against the Old Prussians. They then annexed Pomerelia, the name of the territory of the Polish Corridor of modern Poland, in 1309, which then, as with modern Poland, had formed Poland's access to the sea."

"That sounds curiously reminiscent of current events," commented Elizabeth.

"Indeed. But the date was 1309, not 1939. It was a significant event. By the fourteenth century, the Germans, via the Holy Roman Empire, had re-established control over almost all of their original prehistoric homelands. In 1335, Silesia, which had previously been under Polish rule, became part of Bohemia, and thereafter became increasingly bound to the Holy Roman Empire. It passed to the Hapsburgs in 1526, and became part of Prussia in 1742. Control was followed by settlement, as large numbers of Germans settled in the east, especially in Pomerania, Silesia and Prussia. The Germans called it the Ostsiedlung, or eastern settlement. They built scores of castles and market towns across these territories, establishing a civic society with organised commerce, industry and agriculture, which the Slavs had not been capable of. Apart from their aristocracy, the Poles and other Slavs were mostly still living in conditions little changed since the late Iron Age. Their main advantage at this time was in numbers, with Slavs still forming the majority of the population in many of the rural areas of these provinces."

"So the eastern border at this time was not greatly different from Germany's eastern border in 1914," observed Mary.

"That's right, except that Prussia and Pomerelia were outside the territory of the Holy Roman Empire proper, belonging to the Teutonic Order. This situation continued with little change for a further century; but then in 1410, the Teutonic Knights suffered a disastrous defeat at the Battle of Tannenberg. In 1386, Poland and Lithuania had formed an alliance, mainly against the Teutonic Knights of Prussia, and in 1410 a combined Polish and Lithuanian army attacked Prussia and inflicted a heavy defeat on the Teutonic Knights at Tannenberg.

"The alliance with Lithuania saw a dramatic change in Poland's fortunes. Lithuania itself was already rapidly conquering territory to its south and east, expanding into Russia and Ukraine. The Polish-Lithuanian Commonwealth, as the alliance was known, became one of the most powerful states in Europe over the following two centuries, expanding to reach the Black Sea, having absorbed all of Ukraine, and even taking Moscow in 1610.

"In 1453, there was a major uprising in Prussia against the rule of the Teutonic Knights. The rebels sought the assistance of the King of Poland. The Poles forced the Teutonic Knights to capitulate under the Treaty of Thorn in 1466. Under the treaty, Pomerelia, Danzig, Thorn and Kulm – essentially the Polish corridor – were returned to Poland; parts of Prussia itself were ceded to Poland; and what was left of Prussia became a vassal territory of the Polish crown. The Teutonic Order never really recovered from this blow, and in 1525 the Order relinquished control of what was left of Prussia to a secular Duke, who remained a vassal of the Polish Crown. Thereafter, the Order largely faded from history.

"Poland was now at the zenith of its power, and this continued over the next couple of centuries, although the boundary of the Holy Roman Empire with Poland held firm, indicating that the area within the Empire was now definitely German. The seventeenth century saw the start of Poland's decline towards its eventual demise. In 1648, there was a major rebellion by Cossacks in Ukraine, with the rebels appealing to Russia for assistance. A series of wars with Russia saw a major loss of territory by Poland to Russia. This was followed by a series of invasions by Swedish armies, which devastated much of Poland. Sweden was another power which, like Russia, was also in the ascendant during this period. In 1657, the Duchy of Prussia, taking advantage of Poland's weakened state, threw off its vassal status and became a sovereign state again, with close links to Brandenburg in the Holy Roman Empire. The eighteenth century saw a continued decline of Poland, with further losses of territory to Russia. Poland's decline was such that by the late eighteenth century, the neighbouring powers of Russia, Austria and Prussia were able simply to grab territory in what became known as the 'partitions of Poland', between 1772 and 1795. With the last of these partitions, in 1795, Poland ceased to exist. By far the largest share was taken by Russia. Most of Poland's vast expansion in the fourteenth and fifteenth centuries had been to the east and southeast, resulting in Polish rule over huge areas populated by non-Polish people, especially White Russians and Ukrainians. Many in Russia saw the partitions of Poland as the liberation of these people from Polish rule. That's a point we will be coming back to later on."

"Again, curiously reminiscent of current events," said Elizabeth.

"Indeed," said Geoff. "I think the significance of what's just happened will form a major piece of evidence for this inquiry." He continued: "The final partition of Poland in 1795 was immediately followed by the Napoleonic Wars, which saw the territory of what had been Poland occupied by French forces in 1807. Napoleon created a vassal state, the Grand Duchy of Warsaw, which only existed until 1813, when it was overrun by Russian forces pursuing what was left of the French army after its defeat at Moscow.

"The Congress of Vienna of 1815 essentially created the Europe into which all of us were born. The continental powers were Prussia – the German Empire after 1871 – Russia, Austria-Hungary and France, once France was rehabilitated under the Bourbons. Poland, or most of it, was part of the Russian Empire, with the remaining bits shared between Prussia and Austria. Most significantly, Pomerelia, Danzig, Thorn and Kulm – in other words, the former Polish corridor – was confirmed as being part of Prussia, as also were the city and district of Posen." He indicated the areas on the map. "Apart from this, Congress Poland, as part of the Russian Empire, was strictly confined to the Polish-speaking areas of Europe only.

"As far as Poland and Germany were concerned, the following century saw no fundamental change. The borders remained unchanged, while constitutionally, all of Prussia became part of the German Empire after the defeat of France in the war of 1870-71. The Germanisation of the Prussian areas of the former Poland continued throughout the century, with Germans becoming a majority in the former Polish corridor, including Danzig, by 1914. Poles continued to form a minority in most parts of eastern Prussia, but only in the Posen district and some districts in eastern Silesia and east Prussia did they continue to form a local majority.

"In Poland itself, it took a while for them to accept their status as part of the Russian Empire. As originally constituted under the Congress of Vienna, Poland was a kingdom, united with Russia through the Tsar, who also held the title of King of Poland. In 1830, there was a major uprising in Poland against Russian rule, and for a while the Russians lost control of most of Poland. It was several months before the Russian army was able to crush the rebellion and re-establish control over the country. Thereafter, the Kingdom of Poland lost most of the autonomy it had previously enjoyed, including its constitution, army and legislative assembly, and it was integrated more closely into the Russian Empire."

"I think that was the rebellion for which Chopin raised

money through benefit concerts in Paris," said Mary.

"Indeed," said Geoff, "it was widely supported by Polish exiles abroad, such as Chopin; and many more Poles went into exile following the failure of the rebellion. A further, much weaker rebellion took place in 1863, which was put down by the Russians without much difficulty. The Kingdom of Poland, which had continued to exist as a nominal entity after the rebellion of 1830, was abolished altogether, and Poland was fully integrated into the Russian Empire. By the late nineteenth century, most Poles accepted the status quo, as Poland saw a considerable development of modern manufacturing industry, railways and commerce as part of the Russian Empire. Many of those who didn't, and who remained antagonistic to Russian rule, emigrated to the United States. This period saw the height of European emigration to America, and many thousands of people emigrated from Poland during this period.

"This brings us up to the Great War and the creation, in its aftermath, of modern Poland. We'll take a break, as this is a convenient point at which to interrupt the narrative. After the break, we'll go into the creation of modern Poland in some detail."

Ten

The presentation continued with Geoff now focusing on the volume of research that he and Sylvia had done relating to modern Poland.

"When we think of the Great War from an English perspective," Geoff began, "that perspective is inevitably dominated by the Western Front, the history of which is only too familiar to us all. For most people in England – and perhaps I should now say the British Isles – the details of what happened on the Eastern Front tend to be much less familiar. In many ways, the Eastern Front was almost a separate war, and one which was fought over a much larger area than the Western Front.

"After a brief incursion into eastern Prussia in August 1914, the Russians suffered a significant defeat at the Battle of Tannenberg, and thereafter the Germans began pushing the Russians steadily, if somewhat slowly, back into Poland. Further south, the Russians initially had better fortunes against the Austrians in Galicia, taking Przemysl in March 1915. German reinforcements quickly turned the tide against the Russians, who lost Przemysl in late May, and by mid-1915 the Russians were in full retreat along the whole front. Warsaw fell to the Germans on 5th August 1915, and by late 1915 the whole of Poland was in German hands.

"One consequence of this was that Poland was not directly affected by the Russian revolution, since it was well behind the German lines by that date. Although the revolutionary government in Russia led by Kerensky maintained the alliance with the Western Allies, the Russian army was now in a parlous state, with large-scale desertions, and the German advance accelerated. However, when the Bolsheviks seized power in November 1917, a dire situation turned into a catastrophe when the Bolsheviks refused to continue the war, and the whole Russian front collapsed.

"The Bolsheviks proposed a peace treaty to the Germans, and after a ceasefire was agreed in December 1917, negotiations began at Brest-Litovsk, which by that time was well behind German lines. The assumption by the Bolsheviks that a peace treaty would preserve the boundaries of the former Russian Empire was quickly disillusioned. Poland, Lithuania, Latvia and large areas of Ukraine were already in German hands, and much of the rest of Ukraine was in revolt against Russian rule. The Germans made it clear that it was their intention that Ukraine would become independent, and that Poland and the Baltic states would be within the German sphere of influence – essentially vassal states of Germany. Poland would retain the boundaries of Congress Poland. The Bolsheviks refused to sign such a treaty, so the German army resumed its advance eastward, quickly overrunning huge areas of territory, including all of the rest of Ukraine, and almost reaching Petrograd. The Bolsheviks capitulated and signed, which cleared the way for the great German spring offensive on the Western Front.

"The Armistice of November 1918 transformed the situation on the Eastern Front. The Western Allies backed the independence of Poland, Estonia and Latvia as fully sovereign countries, not as vassal states of Germany. They also supported forces fighting for the independence of Ukraine. Germany was required to hand the Polish Corridor and the city and district of Posen over to the newly independent state of Poland, which had been declared by Polish nationalists within a few days of the Armistice. Following the disintegration of the Austro-Hungarian Empire, Western Galicia," he indicated the area on the map, "was also awarded to Poland by the Allies. Eastern Galicia," he again indicated, "was allocated to Ukraine, but it was immediately claimed by Poland.

"This last point highlighted a dilemma for the Western Allies, although the nature of the dilemma was not always appreciated. After the Bolsheviks seized power in Russia, the Allies first of all tried to remove them by direct military intervention, in places as far apart as Murmansk and Vladivostok. The intervention which came nearest to success was actually the one in Vladivostok, in which the Czech Brigade fought their way right across Siberia – half way round the world – and into European Russia, getting to within 200 miles of Moscow before having to turn back. It was one of the greatest untold campaigns of military history. Eventually all these interventions failed. If the Allies were unable to get rid of the Bolsheviks, one way of limiting their power was to reduce as far as possible the territory they controlled, by supporting the independence of countries such as Poland, Estonia and Latvia, which used to be part of the old Russian Empire. It was the case of Poland in particular which illustrated the ultimate folly of this policy, creating far more problems than it solved, and, as we have just seen, leading to most of these territories falling to the Bolsheviks anyway. The details of how the Polish state came into being form an important part of the evidence of this inquiry, because this is the state which Chamberlain has taken Britain to war with Germany over.

"The Versailles Conference in 1919 established the Commission on Polish Affairs to try and establish internationally agreed boundaries for the new Polish Republic. In the Commission's initial report of that year, the most important feature was the Curzon Line, defining Poland's eastern boundary. This fairly closely followed the ethnic boundary of the territory inhabited by ethnic Poles, and wasn't much different from the boundary of Congress Poland. In fact, the Commission proposed that the boundaries of the new Poland should essentially be those of Congress Poland, with the addition of western Galicia, which was also ethnically Polish, and the districts taken from Germany, mainly the Posen district and the Polish Corridor. In 1919, many saw this as quite an optimistic proposal, since at that time it looked doubtful as to whether Poland would be able to resist annexation by the Bolsheviks.

"Although the Versailles Conference made proposals about the future of Eastern Europe, the Conference had a very limited ability to influence events there. Unlike in Western Europe, where the war and the fighting ended abruptly with the Armistice, in Eastern Europe, the war, and the fighting, never really stopped; or rather, it became a different war. The war of Germany and Austria-Hungary against Russia was replaced by a series of wars of independence as the new states, which had formerly been part of the Russian Empire, sought to establish themselves. As well as fighting against the Bolsheviks, who were trying to establish their control over all the territory of the former Russian Empire, the new states were also fighting each other over possession of disputed territories.

"Poland was heavily involved in the fighting in Eastern Europe, which, as I indicated, consisted of several separate wars going on at once. The ultimate outcome of these wars not only defined the shape of Eastern Europe for the following two decades, but also, as we have seen, formed a major factor in the causes of the present war.

"One of the first consequences of the Armistice of 11th November 1918 was that the Bolsheviks renounced the Treaty of Brest-Litovsk, under which they had been forced to accept the loss of Poland, the Baltic states and Ukraine to the German sphere of influence, as well as

Finland. Bolshevik forces immediately began pushing into Poland, the Baltic states and Ukraine. Initially they were successful, advancing more than 200 miles over a long front. Lithuania, which has a significant part in this narrative, had attempted to establish its independence in 1918, initially under German auspices, then as a fully independent state after the Armistice. This was quickly attacked by the Bolsheviks, who were determined to re-establish control over all the territory of the former Russian Empire. By January 1919, the Bolsheviks had taken Vilnius and Pinsk, and further south, had overrun most of Ukraine, including Kiev. It wasn't until late February 1919 that the Bolshevik advance was stopped and, in late March, a counter offensive was launched by the Poles and the Lithuanians. The Bolsheviks were pushed back, and on 19th April, the Poles captured Vilnius. Up to this point, the Poles and the Lithuanians had been fighting as allies against a common enemy, the Bolsheviks. However, the Poles proved to be duplicitous, as the Lithuanians now discovered. Led by Pilsudski, the Poles had ambitions to create a Greater Poland, incorporating vast territories to the east of Poland proper, either as part of the Polish state, or as vassal states under Polish hegemony. These included the three Baltic states, White Russia, and most – if not all – of Ukraine. Needless to say, any such idea was fiercely opposed by these nations, which were fighting for their own independence.

"Once Polish intentions became clear after the capture of Vilnius, which was the ancient capital of Lithuania, fighting broke out between the Poles and the Lithuanians, which quickly developed into a full-scale conflict. The Lithuanians were always at a disadvantage militarily, having much smaller forces. Nevertheless, they managed to prevent the Poles from overrunning all of Lithuania and annexing it, even if they were unable to retake Vilnius. They were also at a disadvantage diplomatically, since the Western Allies refused to recognise Lithuanian independence. The Allies, through the agency of the Conference of Ambassadors, proposed ceasefire lines in June and July 1919. The Lithuanians accepted the second line, known as the Foch line, after the French general, even though it meant giving up even more territory to the Poles, in the hope that this would lead to Allied recognition of Lithuania, although that didn't happen. The Poles continued to grab territory until the front stabilised in August and fighting died down. Having failed to take Lithuania militarily, the Poles then tried to organise a coup d'etat in Lithuania, to install a puppet government which would agree to Lithuania being absorbed into a Greater Poland. The Lithuanians detected the coup plot, however, and it was successfully foiled. Thereafter, the situation died down until the following year.

"Meanwhile, the Poles had been busy elsewhere. Among the many nations in Eastern Europe who were seeking independence in a state of their own at the end of the Great War were the Ukrainians. For most of its history, the territory of Ukraine has been ruled by its more powerful neighbours, especially Russia and Poland. During the zenith of Polish power, from the fifteenth to the seventeenth centuries, almost all of Ukraine was part of Greater Poland. Much of southern Ukraine then came under Ottoman rule, and was only freed from that when it was conquered by the Russians in the eighteenth century. In the partitions of Poland in the late eighteenth century, most of Ukraine which had been under Polish rule went to Russia, while Austria took eastern Galicia, Ruthenia – which became the easternmost tip of Czechoslovakia after the Great War – and the Bukovina district, which is now in Romania. This division of Ukraine between Russia and Austria had its consequences when Ukrainians tried to establish their own independent state at the end of the Great War. After the first Russian revolution in 1917, a Ukrainian Republic was declared. After the Bolshevik revolution, it declared its independence as the Ukrainian People's Republic. After the Treaty of Brest-Litovsk, this was occupied by the Germans, who replaced it with a puppet state under German control. The Ukrainian People's Republic was re-established after the German surrender, but the Bolsheviks refused to recognise Ukrainian independence and attacked it. In February 1919, the Bolsheviks seized Kiev, and most of Ukraine dissolved into general violence and disorder. Meanwhile, the Austrian areas of Ukraine declared a separate independence as the West Ukrainian People's Republic in November 1918, on the collapse of the Austro-Hungarian Empire. This was immediately attacked by the Poles, who had plans to incorporate Ukraine, or as much of it as possible, into a Greater Poland. In the ensuing war, the Poles were ultimately successful, being better organised and better equipped, including with tanks supplied by the French – although the French protested that these had been supplied for use against the Bolsheviks, not the Ukrainians. By August 1919, the Poles had overrun almost all of the territory of the West Ukrainian People's Republic, as far as the border with eastern Ukraine, most of which fell to the Bolsheviks with the defeat of Denikin's White forces later that year. The West Ukrainian People's Republic ceased to exist, and its Government went into exile in Vienna.

"In late 1919 and early 1920, the fighting died down somewhat, and the front stabilised. Poland was now in possession of vast territories to the east of Poland proper: a large part of Lithuania, including its ancient capital, Vilnius; most of White Russia, including its capital, Minsk; and most of western Ukraine. But Pilsudski still wasn't satisfied. In particular, he wanted the rest of Ukraine, either as part of Greater Poland, or as a vassal state of Poland. He envisaged a Polish sphere of influence – effectively an empire – stretching from Finland to the Caucasus, with Russia reduced to backwardness and poverty, cut off from the Baltic and Black Seas, and most of its natural resources.

"In early 1920, Pilsudski prepared for a great offensive against Soviet Russia to achieve this aim. In April 1920, Pilsudski signed a treaty with Symon Petliura, the former leader of the Ukrainian People's Republic, to give a veneer of legitimacy to the attack. Petliura was in exile in Poland, as almost all of eastern Ukraine had been overrun by the Bolsheviks. Petliura was hoping that Polish assistance would enable him to re-establish an independent Ukraine.

In reality, Pilsudski had no intention of allowing Ukraine to become anything other than a vassal state of Poland. On 24th April 1920, the Poles launched their offensive into eastern Ukraine, with the objective of bringing all of the rest of Ukraine under Polish control. Initially, the attack was successful, with large areas of territory being overrun as the Bolsheviks fell back. On 7th May, the Poles captured Kiev, the Ukrainian capital. Polish forces then crossed the river Dnieper; but thereafter, the offensive stalled. The Poles now had a huge area of territory behind their front line, and as well as being distant from their supply bases, they were finding that they simply didn't have the resources to control such an area of territory. The Polish army had only been re-established a couple of years earlier, and much of it was still makeshift. Another factor was that Petliura's Ukrainian forces, who were with the Poles, didn't receive the expected support from the Ukrainian population. Many Ukrainians, as well as being weary of war and fighting generally, were suspicious of the alliance with Poland, and of Polish intentions for Ukraine. Pilsudski's ambitions were proving to be greater than his resources.

"On 24th May 1920, the Bolsheviks counter-attacked, and because they now outnumbered the Poles by a considerable margin, they quickly started pushing the Poles back. On 13th June, they retook Kiev, and continued pushing the Poles back. The Bolsheviks were also advancing further north, into White Russia, and into Lithuania. By this time, the Lithuanians, who had been fighting against the Bolsheviks alongside the Poles in 1919, had realised that it was the Poles who were their principal enemy, and in 1920 they were fighting alongside the Bolsheviks. On 12th July 1920, a peace treaty was signed between Lithuania and Soviet Russia, under which Soviet Russia recognised Lithuania's independence, with Vilnius as its capital. This was of major significance to the Lithuanians, as the Western Allies were still refusing to recognise Lithuania, since they favoured the Poles. This was essentially an act of expediency by the Bolsheviks, who still harboured longer-term designs to incorporate Lithuania into Soviet Russia; but it gave the Lithuanians the diplomatic break they needed in a desperate situation, and it eventually led to wider diplomatic recognition. On 14th July, the Bolsheviks captured Vilnius from the Poles, and Lithuanian forces reached the city the following day. Over the next couple of weeks, the Lithuanians took the Suwalki region, an area at the southern tip of Lithuania, from the Poles. Meanwhile, the main Bolshevik advance had pushed deep into Poland. By early August, Bolshevik forces had advanced almost as far as Danzig, and were threatening to surround Warsaw. The Poles were desperately appealing to the Western Allies for assistance. They agreed to a proposal that Poland's eastern border should be the Curzon Line, and that Vilnius should belong to Lithuania, in return for promises of Allied assistance. In fact, not much assistance was sent in the end. One reason was that in Britain, dock workers refused to handle cargos that would provide any assistance to the Poles against the Bolsheviks. There was a lot of sympathy for Soviet Russia on the Left in Britain, including among many trade unions."

"Yes, I remember that," commented Mary. "Although at the time, I didn't really understand what was going on, so it's interesting that you mentioned that."

"Even Lloyd George wasn't over-keen on the Poles by that time; but the prospect of a Bolshevik-controlled Poland was even more alarming," said Geoff. "In the event, the assistance wasn't needed. On 15th August, after launching their bid to take Warsaw, the Bolshevik Red Army suffered an unexpected and catastrophic defeat. Although most people aren't aware of it, this was one of the most decisive battles of recent times. Had the Red Army won, and completed its conquest of Poland, the course of history would have been very different. As it was, the Red Army fell back in disorder, such was the scale of its defeat. When an armistice was finally agreed between Poland and the Soviets in October, it was as much because of the exhaustion of the Polish army as for any other reason. The armistice left the Polish eastern front more or less where it had been when they launched their assault against the Soviets six months earlier in April. The terms of the armistice were finalised in the Treaty of Riga, signed on 18th March 1921, which fixed the Polish-Soviet border. The treaty was a final betrayal of the Ukrainians, to whom the Poles had previously given an undertaking not to sign a separate peace with the Bolsheviks. Under the treaty, Ukraine was partitioned between Soviet Russia, which took central and eastern Ukraine, and Poland, which took western Ukraine and incorporated it into Poland. Petliura and the remnants of his army in eastern Ukraine were quickly routed by the Bolsheviks and driven into Poland, where they surrendered to the Poles. Petliura eventually went into exile in Paris.

"By the time the Treaty of Riga was signed, the Poles had used their military to settle another aggression against one of their neighbours in their favour. As they pushed the Red Army back after its defeat outside Warsaw, Polish forces began invading Lithuania. They seized the Suwalki region from Lithuania in September. The League intervened in the dispute over the Suwalki region and arranged a settlement in Poland's favour. But despite this, Polish forces continued to attack Lithuania, to grab as much territory as possible, if not to overrun the whole country.

"The dispute over the Suwalki district," he turned and indicated the place on the map, "was settled by a peace agreement supervised by the League. The Suwalki district had been part of Lithuania continuously from the thirteenth century down to the partitions of the late eighteenth century, when it became part of Russia. The Lithuanians therefore regarded it as part of Lithuania, although by the twentieth century it had a mixed population of Lithuanians, Poles and ethnic White Russians, with the White Russians probably being the largest component. Despite this, the Lithuanians agreed to the district becoming part of Poland, in the interests of a wider peace settlement. But despite being granted Suwalki by the League, and having signed a peace agreement with Lithuania, the Poles were still not satisfied. Aware that their militarism was giving them an increasingly bad reputation, the Poles now staged a crude trick. The day after the peace agreement with Lithuania was signed, the Polish general in charge of Polish forces along the border with Lithuania, General Zeligowski, staged a fake mutiny against the Polish Command. It later emerged, however, that this was secretly agreed with Pilsudski. Zeligowski then invaded Lithuania with the forces under his command, the objective being the Lithuanian capital, Vilnius, which Zeligowski's troops seized the following day. The Lithuanians were outnumbered and continued to be pushed back, with Zeligowski's forces threatening to take Kaunas, the provisional capital, before the Lithuanians were able to halt the Polish advance. A ceasefire was arranged by the League on 30th November. Meanwhile, Zeligowski had proclaimed what he called the Republic of Central Lithuania, with Vilnius as its capital and himself as its provisional ruler. This was very obviously a puppet state of Poland, which was confirmed just over a year later in early 1922, when the 'parliament' of the Republic of Central Lithuania voted for the republic to be incorporated into Poland. A month later, it was incorporated into Poland, and this was recognised by the League in March 1923.

"So, within a few months of promising the Allies to accept the Curzon Line as their eastern boundary, and to respect Lithuania's territorial integrity, the Poles had seized vast territories to the east of the Curzon Line, including the Lithuanian capital, and large areas of Ukraine and White Russia, leaving millions of non-Polish people under Polish rule. Does that kind of behaviour by a state remind you of anything that's happened very recently? I put it that way because it's a point we shall be returning to in due course."

The presentation was adjourned for lunch at that point. After lunch, the presentation was continued by Sylvia, who had focused her research particularly on recent historical events.

"As we have already heard, from its inception, the new Polish Republic has been characterised by aggression against most of its neighbours," she began. "Lithuania has been a particular victim of this. Following the seizure of Lithuania's capital, Vilnius, by the Poles, Lithuania broke off all contact with Poland, as the Lithuanians regarded Poland as virtually being in an undeclared state of war against Lithuania. All trade, communications, even mail links with Poland were broken. This continued for most of the next twenty years. Then in March 1938, taking advantage of the fact that international attention was focused on the German annexation of Austria, the Poles issued an ultimatum to Lithuania. The Poles demanded that Lithuania grant diplomatic recognition of Poland. This was to try and force Lithuania into accepting that Vilnius was part of Poland. An additional demand was that Lithuania open up its transport and communications facilities to Polish goods. The Poles wanted additional access to the Baltic through Lithuania's ports, and the Lithuanians suspected – with good reason – that the ultimate objective of Poland was to take control of those ports by incorporating all of Lithuania into Greater Poland. The Poles massed their army along the border, and rather than face immediate annexation by Poland, Lithuania capitulated to the Polish demands. Most Lithuanians opposed the capitulation, but the Lithuanian Government was under no illusions about Poland's ultimate intentions, which were to annex Lithuania. Accepting the Polish ultimatum would at least give them a little more time to prepare Lithuania's defences.

"Emboldened by their success against Lithuania, the Poles stepped up their aggression when the next opportunity presented itself – the betrayal of Czechoslovakia at Munich. Chamberlain in particular induced the Czechs to capitulate, and while most attention was focused on the seizure of the Sudetenland by Germany, much less attention was given to the fact that Poland also seized sizeable areas of Czech territory. The most significant of these was the area known as Czechoslovak Teschen. The Dukedom of Teschen had belonged to the Crown of Bohemia since the fourteenth century, as part of the Holy Roman Empire." She turned and pointed to the place on the map. "Teschen had never been part of Poland in modern times. In the sixteenth century it passed to the Hapsburgs as successors to the Crown of Bohemia, and down to 1918 it was part of the Austro-Hungarian Empire. In 1918 it had a mixed population of Czechs, Slovaks, Poles and Germans. Czechoslovakia declared its independence from the collapsing Austro-Hungarian Empire on 28th October 1918, and claimed all the lands of the former Crown of Bohemia, including Teschen. However, when the Poles declared their republic on 9th November, they also claimed Teschen on the basis of the Polish element in the population, and this led to an immediate dispute with Czechoslovakia. The dispute was referred to the Western Allies. The decision of the Allies was to divide Teschen into two halves, with the western half going to Czechoslovakia, and the eastern half, including most of the city of Teschen itself, going to Poland. The decision of the Allies fixed the border for the time being, but the Poles were still not satisfied and wanted the whole of the Teschen district. Their opportunity came after Munich. On 30th September, the day of the Munich Agreement, the Poles issued an ultimatum to the Czechs – hand over Czechoslovak Teschen, or face war with Poland. The Czechs, having capitulated at Munich after being betrayed by Chamberlain and Daladier, were therefore in no position to contemplate war, and the following day they capitulated to the Polish ultimatum. On 2nd October, the Polish army seized control of Czechoslovak Teschen. Although not as large as the Sudetenland, it was still a sizeable area of territory – about the size of an English county – and unlike the Sudetenland, the majority of its population were Czechs and Slovaks.

"Whatever the rights and wrongs of the Sudetenland issue – and it has been argued that it was unwise for a Czechoslovak state to have been created with such a large German minority – the betrayal at Munich lay in the fact that the Czechs, having been led to believe that Britain and France would come to their assistance to deter German aggression, had not prepared for war, and so when they were betrayed, they had no option but to capitulate. The seizure of Czechoslovak Teschen was followed by further seizures of Czechoslovak border territory by Poland in December 1938. Hungary also seized border districts of Czechoslovakia at this time. But Hungary is an ally of Germany, and presumably not even Mr Chamberlain could justify a war with Germany in respect of Hungarian interests.

"That brings us into the current year, and brings our presentation up to date, therefore. Bob and Mary will take us through an analysis of current events; but an understanding of the historical background to those events is an essential part of the evidence that this Committee must consider."

Geoff then spoke to sum up.

"This historical part of the presentation has, out of necessity, focused primarily on Poland, because Poland is the reason for the present war. But as you will have seen from our presentation, although superficially the reasons for Britain's declaration of war are very similar to those of August 1914, in truth, the situation this time is very different. The Poland of 1939 is very far from being the Belgium of 1914. Since its creation in the 1830s, Belgium has lived at peace with all its neighbours without conflict or aggression of any kind on Belgium's part. There could hardly be a greater contrast with Poland, which, even in the brief twenty years of its modern incarnation, has waged war against most of its neighbours, and seized large areas of territory from most of them by force or duplicity. In terms of the morality of international law and international relations, there is, in truth, little to choose between Hitler's Germany and the Polish republic. But this is the country which Mr Chamberlain has taken Britain to war with Germany to defend. But as this historical perspective has shown, whatever the reasons for that decision, morality can hardly have been one of them."

Eleven

The presentation was adjourned for a couple of days due to Robert's work commitments, as the next part of the presentation was to be given by Robert and Mary. Given that Robert was working on the sports desk at *The Irish Times*, this meant that he normally had to work on Saturdays and Sundays, and he was therefore given Mondays and Tuesdays off in lieu. On the following Monday morning, therefore, everyone assembled in the Committee Room, as the drawing room was now being called.

"Much of what I will be saying in this part of the presentation," Robert began, "is based on my impressions of information I was privy to as a result of my position at the Foreign Office. For obvious reasons, I don't have the actual information now – it would have been a serious offence to have copied or retained it – so it's important that you bear in mind that what I say will be influenced by my personal opinions of the matter. Opinions come to the fore in this part of the presentation because attention will be focused not so much on the 'what', as on the 'why'. In other words, rather than what happened, the question is why did it happen?

"Geoff and Sylvia's presentation brought us to the beginning of this year, and the events in Czechoslovakia. The first indication of trouble we had at the Foreign Office was the failure by the Germans to confirm the guarantee of the rump Czechoslovakia, which had been part of the Munich Agreement. In February, an Anglo-French note was sent to the Germans about this. The German reply was non-committal and evasive. By March, we were receiving rumours that the Germans were trying to encourage Slovakia to secede from Czechoslovakia. This was confirmed when, in early March, the Prague Government dismissed the Slovak regional government and ordered the arrest of its members. This event precipitated the crisis. The Prague Government appointed a new administration in Slovakia, but the Slovak Prime Minister, Tiso, and his deputy, escaped from where they were being held, and asserted that they were still the Government of Slovakia. On the 13th March, Tiso went to Berlin, and when he went back to Slovakia the following day, he proclaimed Slovakia's independence. German troops were massing on Czechoslovakia's now indefensible borders, and it was clear what would happen if the Czechs tried to intervene. It was a fait accompli, and the Czech President, Dr Hacha, went to Berlin on 15th March to seek terms from Hitler. By the time he got there, German forces had already started to invade the Czech state, and fighting had broken out. Dr Hacha was told that if he didn't immediately accept the German ultimatum, the Czechs would be annihilated. Dr Hacha had no choice but to accept the German ultimatum. The Czechs surrendered, and the Czech territory was immediately occupied by German troops, and was proclaimed as the German Protectorate of Bohemia and Moravia.

"Chamberlain and Daladier both took the view that the guarantees given by Britain and France to the rump Czechoslovakia at Munich were now null and void, because with the secession of Slovakia, Czechoslovakia had ceased to exist, even though the secession had clearly been orchestrated by the Germans. Hitler had, in effect, offered them an escape route from the undertakings given at Munich, and both Chamberlain and Daladier took the escape route. On the 15th March, Chamberlain told the House of Commons that the secession of Slovakia 'put an end by internal disruption to the state whose frontier we had proposed to guarantee. His Majesty's Government cannot accordingly hold themselves any longer bound by this obligation.' Chamberlain went on to say about Hitler's actions against Czechoslovakia: 'I have so often heard charges of breach of faith bandied about which did not seem to me to be founded upon sufficient premises that I do not wish to associate myself today with any charges of that character.'

"Two days later, Chamberlain gave a speech in Birmingham, a speech which was the first indication of the event which will probably be central to this inquiry. The speech marked a complete change of tone towards Germany and Hitler. From being accommodating and conciliatory, Chamberlain was suddenly suspicious and hostile. 'Is this the last attack on a small state or is it to be followed by others?' Chamberlain asked, and he went on: 'No greater mistake could be made than to suppose that because it believes war to be a senseless and cruel thing, this nation has so lost its fibre that it will not take part to the utmost of its power in resisting such a challenge if it ever were made.' There could be no clearer departure from the spirit of Munich. Thus Chamberlain prepared the way for what was to follow. On 31st March, just over two weeks later, he made this announcement to the House of Commons: 'In the event of any action which clearly threatened Polish independence and which the Polish Government accordingly considered it vital to resist with their national forces, His Majesty's Government would feel themselves bound at once to lend the Polish Government all support in their power. They have given the Polish Government an assurance to this effect. I may add that the French Government have authorised me to make plain that they stand in the same position in this matter.'

"We will come back to the declaration shortly, but during this period, two or three other events took place which have a bearing on it. On 15th March, the same day that the Germans annexed what was left of the Czech territory, the Hungarians annexed Ruthenia, the easternmost district of Czechoslovakia. The Hungarians had already annexed the border areas of Slovakia, but these were districts with a predominantly Hungarian population. The annexation of Ruthenia, whose population is overwhelmingly Ukrainian, was a straightforward land grab. There was no formal response to this from London.

"Also in March, the Germans issued an ultimatum to Lithuania demanding the return of the port and district of Memel – the Memelland – which had been detached from Germany by the Treaty of Versailles and made an autonomous territory. It was annexed by Lithuania in January 1923, a move which was approved by the Allies, in part as a sop to Lithuania given the loss of their capital, Vilnius, to Poland. However, it has a predominantly German population, and Hitler now demanded that it be returned to Germany. The Lithuanians were in no position to resist, and on 23rd March, they sent a delegation to Berlin formally to cede the territory. German forces occupied it later the same day. Again, there was no response from London, even though this latest development left Lithuania in a very vulnerable position.

"On 7th April, on Mussolini's orders, Italian forces invaded Albania. The Albanian army was small, weak and poorly equipped and organised, and although it put up fierce resistance where it could, it was no match for the Italian forces, and the Italians overran Albania in only a few days. Albania was then annexed as a protectorate of Italy. Once again, there was no response from London.

"During the spring and summer of this year, there was intense diplomatic activity by the Soviets to try and secure an international agreement or alliance to secure the Soviet Union's western frontiers. Essentially there were two possibilities: an alliance with Britain and France, or an agreement with Germany. In April, the Soviet Foreign Minister, Litvinov, proposed a mutual assistance pact between the Soviet Union, Britain and France, with the main purpose of deterring German aggression. It would be open to Poland to join the pact if it wished, but Polish participation was not essential for the pact to be agreed. It was rejected by both Britain and France. Why it was rejected still isn't clear. Had it been accepted, it's probable, even highly probable, that there would not now be a war. In the event, it's now clear that the Soviets, having been turned down by Britain and France, immediately began sounding out the possibility of an agreement with Germany. The talks with the Germans evidently made rapid progress. By August, this was sufficiently clear to the British and French Governments that they attempted to revive their talks with the Soviets. But by this time, the Soviets were undoubtedly suspicious of British and French motives, and in consequence, the Soviet attitude had hardened. In particular, the Soviets now insisted that Poland was involved in the process, and that the Poles would have to agree in advance that, if attacked by the Germans, they would allow Soviet troops to enter Polish territory in order to confront the Germans. This the Poles absolutely refused to do. The British said that Polish agreement to this was essential, but that the Soviets should proceed on the basis that they would hope that the Poles would ask for Soviet assistance if they were attacked by Germany. This was clearly unrealistic, and it was increasingly obvious to the Soviets that the main intention of Britain and France was now to try and string out the negotiations for as long as possible in order to delay or abort the possibility of a German-Soviet pact. As we now know, the Soviets had no intention of being strung along in this way. Negotiations with the Germans led to the Molotov-Ribbentrop Pact of 23rd August.

"The response of the British Government was to sign the Anglo-Polish Treaty on 25th August. Although this was a mutual defence agreement, in reality it was a unilateral and unconditional guarantee by Britain to Poland. During the negotiations with the Soviets over the summer, it was suggested by a number of people, including by Lloyd George in Parliament, that the Poles should be told that unless they agreed to Soviet troops entering Poland if the Germans attacked, Britain would wash its hands of the matter, and the Poles would be left on their own. This advice was ignored, and instead, Chamberlain gave an unconditional guarantee to Poland. As we now know, Poland was too weak even to defend itself, let alone render any assistance to Britain, and geography dictated that there was no possibility of Britain being able to give any direct assistance to Poland. In effect, given German intentions, the treaty was simply a recipe for war between Britain and Germany.

"Those, then, are the main events in terms of what happened. The focus of our inquiry in this case is to ask why they happened. Why did Chamberlain, having capitulated to the Germans in September 1938, suddenly change his tune in March 1939, and offer a military guarantee to Poland? Why was the guarantee given to

Poland and not Lithuania, which, after the German seizure of the Memelland, was arguably in a much more vulnerable position than Poland? Why was the guarantee to Poland unconditional and, in particular, why was it not a condition that the Poles accept Soviet assistance if they were attacked by the Germans? Why was no serious attempt made to form a defensive alliance with the Soviet Union, which clearly there wasn't?

"We'll take a break just now. When we resume, we'll start to look at some of these questions in detail."

Twelve

When the presentation resumed, Robert turned to the first of the questions he had posed before the break.

"This is one of the most important questions before this inquiry. Why did Chamberlain suddenly change his position with regard to Hitler and Germany back in March? On 15th March, following the news of Germany's annexation of the remaining Czech territory, Chamberlain blandly told the House of Commons that the secession of Slovakia dissolved Britain's obligations to a state which no longer existed, and he rejected any suggestion of bad faith on Hitler's part. But two days later, in a speech in Birmingham, he completely changed his tune, claiming that Hitler was now a menace to the smaller states of Europe, and to European peace, and making a clear threat that Britain would be prepared to take action against Germany.

"Why? Nothing had changed objectively in those two days. If Chamberlain saw on the 17th March that Hitler was a threat to European peace, he could have seen that just as clearly on the 15th, when he gave his bland assurances to the House of Commons. Two weeks later, as we have seen, came the guarantee to Poland. That must have been decided at the time of Chamberlain's Birmingham speech. The subsequent two weeks were needed to organise a coordinated response with France, which gave the same guarantee at the same time. The guarantee to Poland is a strong indication that this was not simply a matter of Chamberlain changing his mind on a whim. A decision must have been made, probably elsewhere in the Government, and Chamberlain went along with it. The guarantee to Poland was a critical decision. It meant that the negotiations with the Soviets over the summer were futile – and were intended to be futile. Britain's policy had already been decided. The linchpin of Britain's security alliance against Germany was to be Poland – the Poland that has now been erased from the map. The guarantee to Poland made war with Germany inevitable. In other words, war with Germany was the intention, and had been for some time. A guarantee to Czechoslovakia at the time of Munich would have brought that war about; but whoever in Government was driving the course towards war decided that that was not the moment. So what changed between September 1938 and March 1939? The answer to that inevitably has to focus on the military situation.

"First of all, a bit of background. At the end of the Great War, Britain's armed forces were among the largest in the world, and the largest they had ever been in British history.

At the end of the war, the British army comprised some five and a half million men. This didn't include Empire and Commonwealth forces. By the end of 1919, following demobilisation, this number had reduced dramatically to about 750,000 men. This peacetime strength declined further during the austerity of the mid-1930s, and by the start of the present war, the British army's Home Army comprised twenty-nine divisions. Against this, the German army, following its rapid expansion after Hitler came to power, comprised, according to intelligence estimates, more than a hundred divisions. However, even in the event of a war, there was no immediate prospect of the British and German armies coming into contact with one another. It would be the French army, assuming that France was involved, which would face the German army on land. At the start of the present war, the French army is thought to have comprised about ninety divisions. Given this – and given that the British army didn't change significantly in size or composition between 1938 and 1939 – the army cannot have been a significant factor in the decision taken in March.

"Very much the same can be said about the Royal Navy. At the end of the Great War, the Royal Navy was the strongest it had ever been, with fifty battleships, 118 cruisers, including nine battle cruisers, 407 destroyers and 137 submarines. After the demobilisation at the end of the war, these numbers also reduced dramatically, to nineteen battleships, fifty-two cruisers, 176 destroyers and sixty-four submarines. This situation changed very little over the next twenty years. The Washington and London naval treaties inhibited the building of new warships, and the Royal Navy went into the present war with a strength little different from what it had been following the demobilisation. Nevertheless, this meant that it was still the largest and most powerful navy in the world. The German navy was far smaller and far weaker in every class of warship. Only in one class did the German navy come anywhere near the strength of the Royal Navy: submarines.

"One thing that was demonstrated by the Great War was that the submarine is now the most powerful weapon at sea. During the Great War, ten British capital ships – battleships and cruisers – were sunk by German U-boats, more than the total number of capital ships sunk by all German surface warships during the war. It wasn't the German battleships that almost cut off Britain's vital supply links in 1917 – it was the German U-boats. Even battleships were forced to retreat in the face of enemy submarines. So it's hardly surprising that the new German navy under Hitler has concentrated on building U-boats. At the time of Munich, the German navy had about forty U-boats in service, and at the start of the present war, they were approaching parity in submarines with the Royal Navy – about sixty U-boats. That's a formidable submarine force – more than twice the number of U-boats the Germans had in 1914. But at the start of the present war, the Royal Navy had fewer destroyers than it had in 1914, to contend with a far stronger U-boat force. And yet, whoever in London was driving the course towards war evidently did not consider this to be a significant factor in the decision to go to war. In other words, this seems to indicate that the navy was not the critical factor in the decision.

"And finally, the air force. And here, I believe, is one of the critical factors involved. The air force followed the same general pattern as the other two services. It reached its peak strength at the end of the Great War in November 1918, but was rapidly reduced to a handful of squadrons in the demobilisation following the end of the war. It remained at this fairly low level throughout the 1920s and up to the mid-1930s. However, from this point, the course of events began to differ sharply from the other two services. The main reason for this was that from the early 1930s, the technical development of aeroplanes and aviation began to change and advance rapidly, and this had significant consequences for the air force and military aviation. Going into some of these technical developments is unavoidable if I'm to explain their significance, but I'll do my best to explain as far as possible in layman's terms. Broadly speaking, in the early to mid-1930s, a new and more advanced type of aeroplane began to emerge. But because aeroplanes are still relatively very new, most people have had little or no awareness of this. Up to the mid-1930s, aeroplanes had not changed fundamentally since the early days of aviation. Almost all aeroplanes were biplanes, and they consisted of a wooden framework covered with fabric or thin sheets of plywood, with the wings being held in place by bracing wires, and with fixed landing wheels. The aeroplane that most of us travelled here to Dublin on in August was of this type. The new types of aeroplane are monoplanes, made entirely of metal, and with a rigid structure which removes the need for bracing wires, and with landing wheels that can be retracted in flight. All this means that the new monoplanes are far more streamlined than the earlier braced biplanes. They can therefore fly much faster, even with the same engine power. But aero engines have also seen rapid development in the last few years, and the combination of new, much more powerful engines with the much more streamlined monoplane designs has resulted in aeroplanes with dramatically improved performance in almost every respect. The Great War showed that relatively small technical advances could give an aeroplane a decisive advantage in air combat. These new monoplane designs are so dramatically superior that they've rendered all the earlier biplane types hopelessly obsolete, and this is especially true of military aircraft. When Germany began to re-arm in earnest in 1935, it quickly concentrated on the new monoplane designs for its air force. The pace of German re-armament was such that by 1938, the Luftwaffe, as their air force is called, had a large and powerful fleet of the new monoplanes, both fighters and bombers. The RAF had barely begun its re-armament programme, and as well as being far smaller than the new Luftwaffe, it was still almost entirely equipped with the earlier biplane types, which are now hopelessly obsolete as military aircraft. It's the details of this new development in military aviation which, I believe, were a critical factor in the decision taken by the British Government in March 1939 to come out openly against Germany, and to set Britain on a course to war with Germany. For that reason, I will need to examine these details, and the particular types of aircraft involved."

At this point, Robert set a board up on an armchair where they could all see it. Attached to the board were a number of sketches of aircraft.

"As I'm going to be discussing particular types of aircraft in this part of the presentation, I've made sketches of the most significant types, copied from an aviation magazine, so you'll have some idea of what they look like.

"The speed of the German re-armament in military aircraft is all the more remarkable because they were starting almost from scratch, having been banned from producing military aircraft by the Treaty of Versailles. From almost nothing, within two or three years, the Germans had established a major aircraft industry, producing many different types of military aircraft in large numbers, including some of the most advanced types in the world. Two of those types are of particular significance: the Heinkel 111 bomber; and the Messerschmitt 109 fighter."

He turned and pointed to two of the aircraft sketches on the board.

"The Heinkel 111 is a long-range heavy bomber, one of the fastest and most advanced in the world. The prototype is thought to have first flown in 1935, and it began to enter service with the Luftwaffe in early 1937. By late 1938, at the time of Munich, it's thought that the Luftwaffe had five or six hundred in service. These bombers are capable of flying from airfields in north-west Germany, round the top of Holland and down the North Sea to London, each with a load of two tons of high explosive bombs, then back to Germany.

"The Messerschmitt 109 is one of the new monoplane fighter aircraft. It has a top speed of well over 300 miles per hour and is one of the most advanced fighters in the world. It's the equal of the British Hurricane, and inferior only to the British Spitfire, and then only marginally." He turned and pointed to the sketches of the two aircraft. "The prototype is also thought to have first flown in 1935, and it first entered service with the Luftwaffe in early 1937, with a number of them being sent to the German air detachments fighting alongside Franco's Nationalists in the Spanish Civil War, where they proved superior to any opposition. By the time of Munich, it's thought that the Luftwaffe had about 600 of these fighters in service.

"The reference to Munich is because of the implications for the military situation of the existence of these aircraft. What would it have meant in terms of the air war if Britain had gone to war with Germany in September 1938, over Czechoslovakia? Remember that, as I mentioned just now, the Germans had some 600 modern fast bombers, each capable of bombing London with up to two tons of high explosive. We've seen from the Spanish Civil War, at Guernica, what modern bombers are capable of."

"And some of us remember the bombing of London in the Great War," said Elizabeth.

"Indeed. Imagine that increased tenfold. Perhaps as much as 1000 tons of high explosive, just on the first day. That's what the Germans were capable of, even at the time of Munich. So what did Britain have to counter that at the time of Munich?

"The counter to such a threat consists of two things: defence and deterrence. The Great War showed that the only effective defence against enemy bombers is fighter aircraft. Things like guns and barrage balloons have a role to play, but in the end, the only effective defence is fighters. In September 1938, the RAF's fighter force consisted almost entirely of the obsolete biplane types that I've just described. These couldn't fly as fast as the Heinkel 111 bombers, and therefore simply could not catch them. The only effective fighter the RAF had was the Hawker Hurricane, the first of its modern monoplane fighters." He turned and pointed to the sketch of the aircraft. "At the time of Munich, of the RAF's twenty-five fighter squadrons, only five were equipped and operational with the Hurricane. The other twenty were still flying the obsolete biplanes. However good the Hurricane is, five squadrons would simply have been overwhelmed by the hundreds of Heinkel bombers, even if they had attacked in daylight. Britain's other monoplane fighter, the Supermarine Spitfire," he turned and pointed to the sketch of that aircraft, "was not yet operational with the RAF at the time of Munich. In short, at the time of Munich, the RAF simply did not have the capacity to mount an effective defence against the German bomber force.

"The other counter is deterrence. In this context, deterrence means: 'If you attack us, we will strike back at you in the same way'. The reality was that in September 1938, the RAF was completely incapable of doing that. In September '38, the mainstay of the RAF's heavy bomber force was the Handley Page Heyford."

He turned and pointed to one of the sketches.

"This was a fabric-covered braced biplane with open cockpits and fixed landing wheels. It didn't have the range to reach Berlin from anywhere in Britain. It was an aircraft which was little changed from the bombers of the Great War and by 1938 it was hopelessly obsolete. The German Messerschmitt 109 fighters would have shot it out of the sky before it got anywhere near a target inside Germany, let alone Berlin. And remember, most of the German fighter force was equipped with 109s by then.

"Three types of modern monoplane heavy bomber have been under development in Britain over the last three years: the Armstrong Whitworth Whitley; the Handley Page Hampden; and the Vickers Wellington."

He turned to the board and pointed in turn to the sketches of the three aircraft.

"At the time of Munich, only the Whitley was in service with the RAF, which had only five squadrons of them operational at that point. Five squadrons would have been totally inadequate to form a deterrent when the Germans had ten times that number of the Heinkel 111 bomber in service with the Luftwaffe. In short, at the time of Munich, the RAF had no effective defence against the German bomber force, and no effective deterrent to counter it. The brutal truth that Chamberlain faced at Munich was that if he had started his war against Germany in September 1938, London would have been reduced to rubble within a week – as would most other large British cities. Hitler knew that, and he knew that Chamberlain knew he knew, which was one reason for Hitler's supreme confidence at

Munich. Quite simply, war with Germany at that point was out of the question."

"But now that war has started, London hasn't been bombed by the Germans in that way," George pointed out.

"That's because the RAF now has both defence and deterrence against the German bomber threat. The period of Munich and the months following saw a desperate scramble to re-arm the RAF with modern aircraft. The pace of that re-armament can be seen by comparing the situation at the time of Munich with the situation in March of this year, when Chamberlain gave his guarantee to Poland. From having five squadrons of Whitleys in September 1938, by the end of March 1939, the RAF had twenty squadrons of modern heavy monoplane bombers in service, including eight squadrons of Whitleys, seven squadrons of Handley Page Hampdens and five squadrons of Vickers Wellingtons. Another seven squadrons had converted to one or other of these types by the end of August this year. That's a formidable force of heavy bombers, and although it's still a lot less than the number of Heinkel 111 bombers in service with the Luftwaffe, in the event of a war because of Poland, a large part of the German bomber force would be engaged against Poland, so the situation in the west would be much closer to parity.

"Likewise with fighter forces: from five squadrons of Hurricanes at the time of Munich, by the end of March this year, the RAF had thirteen squadrons of Hurricanes in service and six squadrons of Spitfires. By the end of August, another four squadrons of Hurricanes and four squadrons of Spitfires were operational.

"Although these forces were now formidable, they were still less than half the size of the equivalent German forces of modern bombers and fighters. So although the situation was greatly improved from September 1938, a prudent leader would not have sought to take Britain to war against Germany when the German forces still had such a superiority in numbers. But that's precisely what Chamberlain did. Having reached some minimum position, he immediately set Britain on a course to war with Germany. Whether that minimum was, or is now, adequate still remains to be seen. The Germans haven't bombed London so far; but as we saw with the Zeppelins and the Gotha bombers in the Great War, early caution in the use of weapons tends eventually to be replaced by unrestrained aggression. The German bomber force is still far larger than the British, and now that Poland is defeated, the whole of it can now be brought to bear against Britain. Also, the British bombers face a much longer and more hazardous flight to Berlin than the flight the German bombers face to London. And although the RAF's fighter defences are greatly improved, as we learned from the Great War, fighter aircraft are really only effective during daylight hours – there's very little defence against bombers operating at night."

"As I can remember," commented Elizabeth.

"Indeed. Imagine how that would be with modern bombers. To summarise this part of the presentation, then, the answer to the question: 'Why did Chamberlain suddenly change his tune in March this year – why March?' seems to be that by March, the military situation, particularly in the air, had improved sufficiently for Chamberlain to risk setting Britain on a course for war with Germany, which is what the guarantee to Poland did. In the next part of the presentation we'll look at two questions: 'Why Poland?' and 'Was going to war over Poland in Britain's interests?'"

Thirteen

"So – why Poland?" asked Robert when the presentation resumed. "Although Chamberlain was clearly thinking of Poland when he referred to the 'small states' of Europe in his speech of 17th March, in fact it's rather misleading to describe Poland as having been one of the 'small states' of Europe. Its population of some thirty million was almost as great as that of England or Italy, and its area of 150,000 square miles was much greater than either; in terms of area it was one of the larger states of Europe. The Polish army had about thirty divisions – slightly larger than the British army, although as recent events have shown, it was no match for the German army. So Poland was one of the main states of Europe. Austria, even Czechoslovakia, with a population of about twelve million, Belgium, Denmark – and I will be coming back to Denmark presently – and perhaps especially Lithuania: these are the small states of Europe. Poland – not really. Another small state that was in the news shortly after Chamberlain's speech was Albania, which was invaded and occupied by the Italians in early April. In terms of foreign aggression, Italy under Mussolini has behaved just as reprehensibly as Germany under Hitler. The invasion of Abyssinia provoked international condemnation, which was ignored by Mussolini. The seizure of Albania was just the sort of aggression against smaller states that Chamberlain was describing in his speech, especially as there are suspicions that Mussolini intends to use occupied Albania as a base for further aggression against Greece. In fact, I raised this question at the Foreign Office at the time, but I was told that Britain has no interest in the fate of Albania, or in seeking any kind of confrontation with Mussolini's Italy. The focus was only on Germany, and Poland.

"As we heard from Geoff and Sylvia's presentation, Poland hardly merits the status of being a just cause over which to take Britain into another Great War with Germany. Its behaviour over the last twenty-odd years has been as egregious as that of Germany under Hitler, if not much more so. Chamberlain's decision to give an unconditional guarantee to Poland therefore can only have been for some other reason. One way of illustrating this is to compare the case of Poland with the situations relating to other countries neighbouring Germany. I'll start with Denmark, which I mentioned just now. There is, potentially, a cause for dispute between Denmark and Germany over the Schleswig-Holstein district of the southern Jutland peninsula," he turned and pointed to the place on the map, "or rather, the Schleswig district in particular, which is the northern half of Schleswig-Holstein. I won't go into the details of the dispute, but in 1866 the Schleswig district, which had been a fief of the Danish crown since the thirteenth century, was annexed by Prussia. In 1871, along with the rest of Prussia, it became part of the German Empire. In 1920 the Allies organised a plebiscite in Schleswig. Northern and central Schleswig, which were predominantly Danish, voted to become part of Denmark. Southern Schleswig was predominantly German, and stayed part of Germany. A new border was fixed to reflect the result of the plebiscite. However, the fact that this left a number of German speaking towns and villages on the Danish side of the border, as well as the fact that the whole of Schleswig had been part of Imperial Germany from 1866 to 1920, could potentially lead to a demand by Hitler that the whole of Schleswig be returned to Germany. How likely that is I don't know, as the number of Germans on the Danish side of the new border is relatively very small; but it remains a possibility, if an unlikely one. But Chamberlain hasn't given a guarantee to Denmark, I would suggest, because there is no evidence that Hitler has any interest in Schleswig, or in Denmark. I certainly never heard anything to that effect at the Foreign Office.

"Next, the Netherlands. In contrast with Poland, if the Germans were to invade and occupy the Netherlands, it would have a major impact on Britain's security, bringing airfields for bombers and naval bases for U-boats much closer to Britain's shores. But the Netherlands is neutral, didn't take part in the Versailles Treaty, and there's no evidence that Germany, even under Hitler, has any territorial claims or hostile intent towards the Netherlands. Belgium is a different case. After the Great War, two small enclaves of German territory were transferred to Belgium under the Treaty of Versailles. However, the guarantee of Belgium's independence under the Treaty of London of 1839 – the same treaty over which Britain went to war with Germany in 1914 – was superseded by the Treaty of Versailles, which now adds to the uncertainty of Belgium's position. But Belgium has opted for neutrality. It pulled out of the Locarno Treaty, and its defensive alliance with France of 1920, so the Belgians have put themselves in that position. However, any German attack on Belgium would almost certainly be part of a larger attack on France.

"Luxembourg also borders Germany, but I don't think it's credible that even Chamberlain would have taken Britain into another Great War with Germany over Luxembourg. Also, there's no evidence that Hitler has any particular designs on Luxembourg – other than, as in 1914, as part of a larger attack on France."

"Now that Britain and France are at war with Germany, that must mean that Belgium is now very vulnerable," observed Geoff. "In other words, the Germans don't really have anything to lose now if they attacked Belgium."

"Indeed, and they would have much to gain if they were able to establish submarine bases on the Channel coast as they did in the Great War. But as in the Great War, an attack on Belgium would be part of a larger attack on France. The Belgians were offered a defensive alliance with

France before the present war started and they chose to turn it down – so they are now, as you say, in a vulnerable situation.

"I'll come back to France in a moment. Just to continue the circuit around Germany's borders. Switzerland's neutrality is almost legendary, and there's no evidence that Hitler has any interest in or designs on Switzerland. In the case of Austria, which is now part of Germany, there is the issue of the South Tyrol district, a small enclave which was detached from what had been the Austro-Hungarian Empire and transferred to Italy by the Allies in 1919. The population of the northern part of this district is German speaking. Had it been attached to another of Germany's neighbours, it could, potentially, be the cause of another Czechoslovakia-type crisis. However, Mussolini is Hitler's principal ally, so it's unlikely that Hitler is going to make an issue of it in this case. And even if he did, it's difficult to imagine even Chamberlain taking Britain to war in support of Mussolini's Italy, especially over a minor border dispute. Yugoslavia and Hungary are also both now border states following Germany's absorption of Austria. I'm not aware of any territorial disputes between Germany and those countries, both of which are currently run by governments favourable to Germany. Czechoslovakia and Poland form part of the main subject of this inquiry. Lastly, there's Lithuania. As we heard earlier, Hitler had already settled accounts with Lithuania in March, by obtaining the return of the Memelland. There's no evidence that I'm aware of that Hitler has any further designs on Lithuania. The main danger to that country continued to be from Poland, which undoubtedly harboured designs on Lithuania's territory, up to annexing the whole country. On a list of small states in Europe vulnerable to an aggressive, powerful and hostile neighbour, Lithuania was high on the list; but Mr Chamberlain evidently had no interest in Lithuania.

"And so, to France. If the fate of any country in Europe affects Britain's vital national interests, that country is France. That being so, British policy towards France should have been to assist and encourage France to become as strong and well-prepared as possible to resist and deter any German attack. This would include giving the French sufficient time to achieve this. It would mean giving them time to extend the Maginot Line as far as the sea, since Belgium doesn't want a defensive alliance; it would mean giving them time to introduce a modern command structure for their army; and it would mean giving them time to build up and re-equip their air force with modern aircraft. Doing that would have been the best way of deterring a German attack on France, and at least delaying a return to the Great War. It probably still wouldn't have been enough to avoid war, since sooner or later, Hitler was always likely to make an issue of Alsace and Lorraine; but it would at least have delayed the onset of war, and made an Allied victory more certain. France is far more important to Britain than Poland, and such a policy would have involved a decision, however regrettable, to leave Poland to its fate when it was attacked by Germany. If Chamberlain was genuinely seeking to avoid, as far as possible, a repetition of the horrors of 1914 to 1918, this is the course of action he would have taken. The course of action he has actually taken is in the national interest of neither Britain nor France. Certainly since March this year, he has committed himself to taking Britain to war with Germany at the earliest possible opportunity, and hustling France into war as well. Britain still isn't prepared for war, and France most certainly isn't. Hence the hastily arranged treaty with Poland, a country which, given its behaviour over the past twenty years, was hardly deserving of our country's blood and treasure, even if we were in a position to do anything to help Poland, which we weren't. It seems clear that the main purpose of the treaty with Poland was to take Britain to war with Germany at the earliest opportunity rather than to help Poland."

George raised a hand.

"Just playing Devil's advocate here. Many would say that Chamberlain had little choice but to take a stand over Poland, given the state of public opinion and the way it's shifted against Germany over the last year or so."

"In the first instance, that's true," said Robert. "But that begs the question of why public opinion has changed in that way, and why the focus of that change has been on Germany, rather than, say Italy, given the particularly egregious behaviour of the Italians in Abyssinia, as well as the annexation of Albania, or even Poland, given their recent treatment of Lithuania. The answer to that is that public opinion is heavily influenced by the press, which in turn closely follows official thinking in these matters. I mentioned the Locarno Treaty just now. At the time, it was widely perceived that British policy was that the treaty would improve relations between France and Germany to the extent that France would abandon its defensive alliances in Eastern Europe, which would force Poland and Czechoslovakia in particular to come to terms with Germany, including, if necessary, ceding territory to avoid war. Even at the time of Munich, the press took the line that the best thing would be a political settlement in which the Czechs acceded to all of Hitler's demands and handed over the Sudetenland, which was the outcome that Chamberlain wanted. Chamberlain's motive was that, however much he might have wanted another war with Germany, he understood very well that in September 1938, Britain simply wasn't ready for war, and the French were even less so. And so, Chamberlain was perceived as the bringer of peace, even though a European war over the Sudetenland was unlikely, because neither Britain nor France was in a position to go to war. Since March, however, the press has not only been increasingly belligerent, but the focus of that has been entirely on Germany, largely ignoring the equally provocative actions of other countries, especially Poland, Hungary and Italy. It's no coincidence that this has closely followed official policy in these matters. In other words, Chamberlain has simply been following an agenda which he himself has largely set."

"What do you think Chamberlain's motives are?" asked Christine.

Robert shook his head.

"I'm not really sure. It may be that he's just misguided. But in my view, it comes down to this: if you're going to do a job, you should make sure that it's done properly. If you're going to oppose Hitler, then make sure your opposition is as solid as it can be before committing it. Chamberlain hasn't done that. He's endangered the security of both Britain and France by rushing them into war before they were ready. But that seems to have been his intention, at least since March."

"Again, playing Devil's advocate here," said Geoff, "what about the proposition that the longer we waited before going to war, the stronger Germany would become, especially militarily, and that Chamberlain was right to go to war sooner rather than later, before Germany became too strong?"

"There is merit in that point," said Robert, "but the main consideration is Germany's strength relative to that of Britain and France, both of which are woefully inadequate, especially in the air. Germany's re-armament has been at maximum capacity for some years, whereas Britain's is only just getting under way, so the gap is likely to decrease over time rather than increase. Also, the importance of completing the Maginot Line to the sea before getting involved in a war with Germany cannot be over-emphasised."

"The French must be feeling very uneasy about that now that they're actually at war with Germany," observed George.

"I believe that frantic attempts are being made to improvise an extension of the line towards the sea; but if Hitler attacks in the West any time soon, such efforts are likely to be ineffective. And unlike in 1914, the German forces won't be divided between two fronts. Hitler's pact with Stalin to keep Soviet Russia out of the war should have concentrated minds in London and Paris, but obviously didn't. In fact, the German-Soviet pact should have been a key reason for not going to war over Poland. The full weight of the German army and, even more significantly, the German air force, can now be thrown against the West."

"It's another piece of evidence in the case against Chamberlain," said George.

"A major piece of evidence. Even without the German-Soviet pact, it would have been prudent to have avoided going to war over Poland. As it is, Chamberlain has been nothing less than reckless.

"In other respects as well, Britain is not ready for war, especially another war with Germany. The economy is still a long way from recovery from the worst effects of the Great Depression. There are still over a million unemployed, and much of industry is still in a weak state. It still needs more time before it will be ready to transition to a war economy that will be a match for Germany's. Running a war economy is a massive drain on a country's financial resources, and it's doubtful whether Britain's finances have yet recovered sufficiently from the Great Depression to be able to withstand the strain of another struggle against Germany on the scale of the Great War. Again, prudence and the national interest would indicate not getting involved in a war unless it became absolutely unavoidable, and meanwhile using the time to prepare all the country's defences. All these factors ought to have weighed in the balance against going to war with Germany over Poland, but clearly didn't.

"And so, I think that brings us to a point where we can draw all the threads of this presentation together, and summarise our conclusions so far. It'll make things clearer if we dedicate a separate day for that, so I suggest that we do that tomorrow."

Fourteen

When they all reassembled in the drawing room the following morning, Geoff took the lead in presenting the summary of the inquiry's findings thus far.

"Although this presentation is only an interim report on our committee's findings, it's a significant one because we're already in a position to examine the most important factors which led to war, and what the alternatives might have been," he began. "The outcome of this war is still unknown, and so the final verdict will have to await that; but the events and circumstances leading to the war are a different matter.

"The main purpose of our inquiry is to establish whether it was necessary or in Britain's best interests to go to war with Germany at this time and over this issue, and whether there were alternative courses of action that might have been followed. As we've heard in this presentation, the territorial dispute between Germany and Poland is an ancient one, with both countries having historical bases for claiming the disputed territory, although the area was inhabited by Germanic people long before it was inhabited by Slavs or Poles. One thing demonstrated by history is that Poland is not one of Britain's strategic interests. From the late eighteenth century down to the Great War, Poland didn't exist, other than as a province of the Russian Empire; but that had no effect on Britain's strategic interests, or on the balance of power in Europe. That's also true now, given that Poland has once again effectively ceased to exist. What does matter to Britain is Germany's pact with Soviet Russia, which means that Germany is not fighting a war on two fronts and can use all its forces against Britain and France.

"In the twenty years since it was re-established as an independent state, Poland's behaviour towards its neighbours has been at least as reprehensible as that of Germany under Hitler, particularly towards its eastern neighbours, as we heard in detail in the presentation. It therefore hardly deserves to be a *casus belli* for another war with Germany. So that leads to the question: why did Poland become the *casus belli* for the war? Putting it another way: why Poland but not Czechoslovakia, since both cases were essentially very similar? As we heard in the presentation, the real reason seems to have been more to do with the military situation at the time, or rather, the Government's perception of the military situation, rather than the merits of the case for either Czechoslovakia or Poland. Indeed, the treatment of Czechoslovakia was particularly outrageous. But as we heard in the presentation, the Government's perception of the military situation is a further indication that, in fact, it's being driven by another agenda.

"Over the last few years, there's been a growing expectation in Britain that another war with Germany was likely. However, it looks increasingly as though this has largely been driven by the press, which has promoted the idea, especially in the last few months, that it's Britain's moral responsibility to 'stand up to Adolf Hitler', and that the first opportunity to do so should be taken. This in turn is largely a reflection of the official view. It's a view which is dangerous and short-sighted, and has led to Britain rushing into a war with Germany as soon as, to judge from appearances, the RAF reached some arbitrary minimum number of squadrons of modern aircraft. In other words, it's been driven by a desire by the Government for war with Germany at the earliest possible opportunity. The consequences of this remain to be seen, but the price for it may be a heavy one.

"Was an alternative course of action possible? As we heard in the presentation, it certainly was, and it was one that could just as easily have won public approval. But in order to appreciate this, it's important to understand that in any war with Germany, Britain and France will inevitably be fighting alongside each other. This is by far the most important consideration. Britain's national interest in this matter is wholly bound up with that of France. This means that any assessment of preparedness for war with Germany should have been made of Britain and France together. Both countries would need to have achieved the maximum possible preparedness for war, both individually and jointly. That would mean the RAF having at least parity in modern bomber and fighter aircraft with the Germans, and the Royal Navy having at least the same number of destroyers as at the height of the Great War, to counter the greatly increased U-boat threat. But above all, it means working with and assisting the French in modernising their air force and their army, and in completing the Maginot Line to the sea, as well as making detailed plans for Anglo-French military cooperation in the event of war with Germany. All these things would take time, perhaps at least a couple of years. Whether as much time as that would have been available is difficult to assess. The expectation must be that war with Germany was inevitable sooner or later, assuming that Hitler would eventually make an issue over Alsace and Lorraine, and demand that they be returned to Germany. How long it would have been before that happened it isn't possible to say. An ultimatum to France about Alsace and Lorraine, making the issue a *casus belli,* would make war with Germany unavoidable at that point. But short of that, war should have been avoided if at all possible, and whatever extra time that gave should have been used to maximise defensive preparations for war. It would have meant not getting involved in the dispute between Germany and Poland, and staying out of the war when Germany attacked Poland. Rather, the example of Poland should have been used to impress on the French the urgent necessity of improving their defences while they still had time. It would also have meant making a serious attempt to conclude an agreement with Soviet Russia – and in particular, taking up Litvinov's offer in April this year of a mutual defence pact, instead of deliberately botching the negotiations with the Soviets. Had all this been done, it's even possible that it might have been enough to have deterred Hitler entirely from war with France, however much he coveted Alsace and Lorraine. In December last year, Hitler signed an agreement with France accepting the existing frontier between the two countries. As long as he maintained that stance in public, he wouldn't lose face if he refrained from making Alsace and Lorraine a *casus belli*. As recently as the 6th of October, in a speech to the Reichstag, he again renounced any claim by Germany to Alsace and Lorraine. But in any event, for Britain and France, preparing for war while – as far as possible – trying to avoid it would have been a far better course of action than rushing headlong into war at the earliest opportunity while being badly prepared for it.

"This summarises, very briefly, the facts of the situation leading to the declaration of war, as our investigation has determined them so far. The significance of these facts will also relate to the outcome of this war, which is as yet unknown. If it turns out to be another Great War, with a loss of life on the same scale, then it becomes very relevant to know why this was thought by the British Government to be necessary because of an abstruse territorial dispute of long standing between two rather unsavoury regimes in Central Europe. What Chamberlain's motives were in seeking such a war remains unclear. Whether it was mere foolishness, or vanity – a desire to be seen to be 'standing up to Hitler' – or something more sinister, will be one of the focuses of our investigations in the coming weeks and months."

Fifteen

In the days following the conclusion of the interim presentation, a number of meetings were held in order to agree on the next stage of the Committee of Inquiry's research. It was now close to Christmas, and still nothing had been heard from Graham Shepherd. It seemed clear that something must have gone wrong, and a meeting was held to discuss the matter and to decide what to do.

"First of all, we need to try and find out what the situation is – what has happened," said George. "Until we do, it's going to be difficult to know what to do for the best."

"But we've already tried to do that, without success," said Mary. "Mike took the risk of going up into Northern Ireland to make the telephone calls."

"To be fair, I only attempted to telephone Graham on that occasion," said Mike. "This time, at the very least, we would have to telephone other people as well before we decided to do anything else. One of them would obviously be Duncan, to see if he managed to get a warning to Graham in time. Also to see if he himself is alright, given that he decided to risk staying in Britain."

"What about our rule about not telephoning each other directly?" asked Christine.

"Well, I think the rule is, except in cases of absolute necessity. Given the predicament that Graham is obviously in, I would say that this is such a case," said Mike. "The point is, as George said, that we won't know how best to help Graham until we know what the situation is, and making these telephone calls is the first step in finding that out."

"What do you suggest?" asked Geoff. "Should the calls be made from here, or are you proposing to go up to that place in Northern Ireland again?"

"In the first instance, I propose to go up to the same place in Northern Ireland again – Forkhill, if I remember," said Mike. "The reasons for doing so are the same as the last time. I imagine it'll be much the same as last time, apart from the weather being a bit more bracing, perhaps."

"Perhaps someone else should go this time," said Geoff. "You've already taken the risk once."

"Well, most of you were on that list, so it would be more risky for you than for me," said Mike. "Besides, having done it once, I'm familiar with the route and the layout of the place. I'd be more than happy to make the trip again."

Geoff nodded. "Well, if you're sure, we all appreciate that."

"I'll plan the trip over the next couple of days, and I'll probably go up on Thursday," said Mike.

***

On the Thursday morning, Mike set off as he had done previously, cycling into Dublin to catch the train up to Dundalk. The weather was calm, but chilly, with a touch of frost. As before, the others had a long and anxious wait for Mike to return. Robert, at least, was occupied during the day by his job at *The Irish Times*, and George had appointments with clients at his accountancy firm that afternoon. However, both of them were home again at their usual time, and there was still no sign of Mike. They began the evening meal at the usual time, however, partly for the sake of the children, who needed regular mealtimes. Mike finally arrived while they were in the middle of the meal. He was cold and famished, and refused to say anything about the events of the day until he had warmed up in front of the fire and eaten the meal that Elizabeth had kept warm for him. After he had finished eating, he settled himself into an armchair beside the fire. He closed his eyes for a few moments before opening them again and looking at the others.

"I'm afraid I have some bad news," he said. "Graham and Ann have both been arrested. My information is that they were arrested on the 28th of August, which was a Monday."

"Ann has been arrested as well?" asked Geoff. "But her name wasn't on the list that Bob saw."

"I know, but that's my information," said Mike.

"What about their two children?" asked Elizabeth.

"Did you manage to speak to Duncan?" asked Robert.

Mike held up his hand.

"Let me tell you what happened in order, from the beginning," he said. He paused for a moment before continuing. "Because I was familiar with the geography of the place from my previous visit, I was able to plan the timing of this visit better. I left Dublin for Dundalk on a later train, so I didn't have to spend as much time in Dundalk. I decided, as before, that the best time to make the telephone calls was early evening. The cycle ride up to Forkhill took rather longer than previously, as it was dark by that time, and also rather chilly. By the time I arrived in Forkhill I was pretty chilled, so the first thing I did was to go into the pub there and warm up by the fire in the saloon bar with a nip of whisky. Once I'd warmed up, I went out again and made my way to the telephone box.

"The first call I made was to Graham's number. The operator made the connection, and I heard the ringing tone. I then heard a series of clicks, and suddenly there was a man's voice on the line – a voice I didn't recognise." As he spoke, Mike produced a piece of paper from his pocket. "I jotted down the conversation afterwards, as nearly as I could remember it. The man just said: 'Hello'; so I said: 'Can I speak to Graham, please?' The man asked: 'Who's speaking?' I said: 'I'm a friend of Graham's – is Graham there please?' He replied: 'No, but if you give me your name and telephone number, I'll ask him to call you back.' I said: 'Is Ann there?' He replied: 'No, she's not.' I then asked: 'Who are you?' to which he replied: 'I'm a friend of Graham's.' I asked: 'If Graham and Ann aren't there, where are they?' 'Oh, they're away at the moment,' he said, 'but if you leave me your name and telephone number, I can get them to call you back.' 'Away where?' I asked. 'Oh, just away visiting friends,' he said. 'I know most of their friends, so if you tell me which friends, I can call them myself,' I said. He didn't respond to that, but then asked: 'Where are you calling from?' 'I'm calling from home. I'll call again later this evening,' I said, and then hung up.

"I had to think quickly about what I would do next. The man I'd been speaking to was undoubtedly either the police or someone from the secret service."

"Do you think the police are occupying Graham's house?" asked George.

"Possibly they may be, but I suspect that all calls to Graham's number are being put through to an office in Scotland Yard, or somewhere like that. That would account for the series of clicks I heard on the line before the call was answered. They would undoubtedly be trying to trace the call, so I had to think about how long I could safely stay there. I still had two other telephone calls to make. I decided to risk it, as it would take a few minutes at least to confirm where the call had been made from, and because Forkhill is a fairly remote place, it would then take some time to organise any action on the ground.

"Having decided to press ahead, I then telephoned Duncan. The telephone was answered by the butler, so I told him to tell Duncan it was Mike Warren, telephoning from Ireland. A minute later, Duncan himself came on the line. I asked him if he had any news of Graham, and he said he hadn't heard anything. I described the telephone call I had just made to Graham's number, and said that it sounded as if the police were in Graham's house. Duncan agreed that it sounded as if that was the case. I asked him if he'd managed to warn Graham about the arrest list, and he said that he had driven out to Graham's house in Essex on the evening of the day Bob had come to warn him, and urged Graham and Ann to leave as soon as possible; but he hadn't heard from them since then. Duncan said he had impressed on them the urgency of the situation, and could only hope that they'd managed to escape in time.

"At that point, I didn't know what I was to discover a few minutes later, so I just said that we had seen no sign of Graham and Ann in Dublin, despite keeping watch and making discreet enquiries. It was therefore a mystery what might have happened to them. I asked Duncan how things were for him, and he said that he'd been keeping a low profile since the start of the war, and so far had not had any trouble.

"Conscious of the fact that the minutes were ticking away, I wished Duncan the best of luck, and said we would try to keep in touch, although we probably wouldn't see each other again until after the war at least. He wished me luck, and I ended the call. I then made the third of the three telephone calls. This was to the White Horse Inn in Ridgewell, the village where Graham and Ann live."

"Oh, I remember that place," said Robert. "Graham and Ann took us for a drink there when we visited them a couple of years ago."

Mary nodded in agreement. "The village is very remote," she said. "I remember we had to walk a long way from the nearest station."

"Graham and Ann took me there for a drink when I visited them last year," said Mike. "It was their local pub, and they knew the landlord there well, which was the reason I decided to telephone the inn. I remember the landlord there, and although he probably wouldn't remember me, there was a good chance that he might have some news of Graham and Ann. And so indeed it proved.

"It was the landlord who answered the telephone. As with the first call I made, I jotted down the conversation afterwards, as far as I remembered it. I told him my name was Mike Warren, and that I was a friend of Graham and Ann Shepherd. I said: 'I've been trying to contact Graham and Ann without success. I've telephoned you in the hope that you might have some news of them.' 'The Shepherds? Oh, well…' He sounded a bit confused. 'Well – they… they were arrested.' 'Arrested?' I said. 'Yes, that's right. It happened back in August, just before the start of the war. A great shock it was – nothing like that had happened in the village before. There were three police cars and a black maria turned up early in the morning. When the Shepherds answered the door, the police pushed their way in and arrested them. Mrs Wilkins, who lives opposite, said she saw Mr and Mrs Shepherd being led out by the police and put into the black maria. She then saw their two children put into one of the police cars, which then drove off. She said she was shocked to see it.' 'Why were they arrested?' I asked. 'Well, I don't know for sure, but rumour has it that it was something political.' 'Can you remember what day it happened?' I asked. 'Let me see – it was a Monday. It was the Monday before the weekend the war started. Early in the morning, it was.' 'Have you heard any news about them since then?' I asked. 'Well, the only thing I've heard is a rumour that Mrs Shepherd is in Holloway prison – but that's just a rumour, mind. As far as I know, no-one from the village has actually been to visit her, so whether that's true or not I don't know. As for Mr Shepherd and the two children, I've not heard anything at all, not even a rumour. The whole thing was quite shocking, and it's still the talk of the village. They were regular customers here, and both nice people – seemed to get on well with everyone, and they'd lived in the village for a good few years, so everyone was shocked when they were arrested like that.'

"I was conscious that the minutes were ticking away," Mike continued, "and as he seemed to have told me all that he knew about what had happened, I thanked him for his help and said goodbye. I'd achieved what I'd set out to achieve, so without further ado I left the telephone box, got on my bicycle and made for the road out of Forkhill which was the shortest distance to the border. I didn't encounter any problems, apart from it being dark and rather chilly, and about forty minutes later I was back in Dundalk. I went into a pub in the town centre to warm up in front of the fire there, and then caught the next train back to Dublin."

There was a pause after Mike finished speaking, which was eventually broken by Elizabeth.

"Once again we're all grateful to you for what you've done, Mike, even if the news you've brought back is very disturbing."

There was general consent at this.

"The landlord said it was the Monday before the war started," said Robert. "That would be Monday the 28th August, as I think you said. But if Duncan went out to Essex to warn Graham and Ann on the evening of the previous Tuesday, when I went to see Duncan, why were Graham and Ann still at their house in Essex nearly a week later? I don't understand it."

"Perhaps they didn't take Duncan's warning seriously," suggested Mary.

"Or perhaps there was some other reason why they couldn't leave. Perhaps one of the children was ill," said Christine.

"Duncan did say it was on the Tuesday evening that he went out to see them?" asked Geoff.

"Oh, yes, he was quite definite about that," said Mike. "And he said he made clear the risk of arrest once the Emergency Powers Act was passed, and that Graham's name was on the arrest list."

"Well, in that case, it doesn't make any sense that Graham at least, was still at the house the following Monday," said Robert. "I simply don't understand it."

"What are we going to do?" asked Mary. "Is there anything we can do, at least from here in Dublin?"

"From here, we're effectively limited to writing letters and making telephone calls," observed Geoff. "Thanks to Mike, we at least now know what has happened."

"What else might we be able to find out from here?" asked George.

"Probably not a great deal, and it wouldn't be easy," Geoff said.

"But from Mike's account, there's now another issue," said Elizabeth. "The two children, Richard and Susan. The landlord of the White Horse said they were taken away in a police car, according to the woman who witnessed it. What's happened to them? If Ann is in Holloway prison, that'll be bad enough; but she'll be worried sick about what may have happened to her children. I'm worried myself, on her behalf."

"Is there any way we might find out what's happened to the children?" asked Mary. "Or indeed, to Graham and Ann?"

After a moment, Mike said: "Rather than trying to make a decision now, I would suggest we all put our thinking caps on until tomorrow evening, and then see what ideas we've come up with about what we think would be the best way forward."

There was general agreement at this suggestion.

Sixteen

The following evening, they assembled again after the evening meal. Mike led off the discussion.

"I've been thinking in the first instance of how we might find out more information about Graham and Ann from here," he said. "As far as letters are concerned, we would have to use this address, or at least the General Post Office on O'Connell Street, because we don't have a *poste restante* address in Northern Ireland, which would be impracticable for obvious security reasons. There would be advantages in going up to Northern Ireland to post letters to England, however. There's a post office in Forkhill, and I saw at least one postbox on the way up there. Letters with a British stamp on them would be less likely to arouse immediate suspicion. We could also make telephone calls from here in Dublin, but we've already established the advantages of going up to Northern

Ireland to do that, even if it is a bit risky. There are one or two other villages just over the border which are listed as having a telephone box in the AA handbook, and which are within cycling distance from Dundalk, if we have to use another telephone box for security reasons.

"In theory, we could seek any information from any source by letter or telephone; but in practical terms, the possibilities are limited. For example, in theory, we could write to the Essex Constabulary to ask them if they have any information about Graham and Ann, but it's highly unlikely that the letter would ever be answered. Realistically, the options are much more limited. For example, we could try contacting friends of Graham and Ann, or people who know them, in the hope that they might have heard some news of them.

"One problem with that is that it might put people who replied to us in danger from the authorities, and they might be reluctant to reply for that reason. That would particularly apply to people who are already in danger, and when I was speaking to Duncan, I decided not to ask him to take the risk of trying to find out more information about Graham and Ann for that reason. Another problem is that any responses we got might be too inconclusive to be of much use, or actually unreliable. We might have no means of knowing the reliability of information we received in that way. I'm not saying we shouldn't attempt to find out more information that way, but we must be aware of the limitations."

"I think the first thing would be to make a list of people from whom we could reasonably expect to receive information if we wrote or telephoned them," said Geoff. "Once we've agreed a list, we then confirm the address or telephone number for each of them. It would then be a matter of deciding on the best way of contacting each person."

"That sounds like a practical way forward," agreed Robert.

The others seemed to agree, but Elizabeth then spoke up.

"There's something more important now," she said. "From Mike's account, there's now another issue, which I think is more important, which is the two children, Richard and Susan. I feel very strongly that we must try to do something for them."

"If we can, yes; but who would we approach to find out any information about them?" asked Robert.

"Do we know which school they go to?" asked Mary. "If we contacted the school, they might have some information."

"I think they go to different schools," said Mike. "The younger child, Susan, is aged about ten, and presumably goes to primary school; but the elder child, Richard, is about twelve, and presumably goes to secondary school. Possibly Susan goes to the village school in Ridgewell; but as for Richard, I don't know."

"If they've been taken away by the police, it may be that other arrangements have been made, such as a local authority institution," said Geoff.

"That thought has occurred to me too," said Elizabeth. "In fact, it's what concerns me most about this. I didn't get much sleep last night thinking about it. The thought of the two children, separated from their parents, and possibly also from each other, trapped in some institution and not even understanding why, distresses me beyond words. I've therefore come to a decision. I've decided to go back to England, to London, to try and find out exactly what has happened, to try and locate the children and, if possible, to rescue them by bringing them back here to Dublin."

For a moment there was a surprised silence, before Mike spoke.

"Elizabeth, are you serious? You must know the risk that going back to England would involve."

"Believe me, I've thought about little else since you told us what you had discovered yesterday," said Elizabeth. "Obviously, I've considered the risk, and many other points as well; but in the end, I decided that this is what I must do, and I'm determined to do it. I couldn't live with myself in the future if I knew I hadn't at least made the attempt to rescue the children when I could, and I know that the longer I leave it, the harder it will be to rescue them. I've made my mind up."

There was a pause before Elizabeth spoke again.

"As far as the risks are concerned, I think that they can be reduced or minimised depending on how I go about this. In particular, instead of going to England directly from Dublin, if I went up to Northern Ireland, to Belfast, and travelled to England from there, I would be less conspicuous as a traveller."

"Even so, there are going to be difficulties and risks whichever route you take," said Mike. "For example, since the start of the war, everyone in Britain has been issued with a National Identity Card, which they have to produce whenever officialdom asks to see it. That's likely to include places like railway stations, and possibly hotels."

"Well," said Elizabeth, "as far as that's concerned, one of the things I've brought with me is my old National Identity Card from the Great War, as well as my passport. If I'm asked to produce it, my idea is to say that I'm having to use this old one from the War because my handbag was stolen, with my new Identity Card in it, and I haven't been issued with a replacement yet."

"Well, that's a good plan at least," said Mary. "But it will be of no avail if your name's been added to the list and they're on the lookout for you."

Elizabeth shrugged.

"That's an inevitable risk if I decide to cross the border," she said. "That's the risk I've decided to take, if it's something that's going to happen anyway. But it may not be, and I might manage to slip through without being noticed. That's what I'm hoping to be able to do."

"There's no way we can talk you out of this, Liz?" Mike asked.

Elizabeth shook her head.

"I was awake most of last night thinking about it, and I'm quite certain in my mind that this is what I must do. As I said just now, I would never be at peace with myself if I hadn't at least made an attempt to rescue the children. All I can do is to ask you to help me to plan this journey in ways that will minimise the risk."

"Well, if it's something you're determined to do, Liz, of course we will," said Mary, "but I'm deeply worried by the idea of your doing this."

"If Liz is determined to do this, then the best thing to do is to help her plan it in a way that minimises the risks involved," said Mike. "Perhaps if we go through the journey stage by stage, we can identify where the risks and problems are most likely to arise, and think of stratagems for dealing with them."

Everyone seemed to agree with this, so after a short break, discussions resumed in earnest.

***

Two days later, plans for the journey had been made, as far as was possible. On the Saturday morning, Mike, Geoff and George had gone into Dublin to buy items for the journey. Geoff managed to buy a gas mask, complete with box and carrying strap, from the Great War, which he found in a junk shop on Cuffe Street, just off St Stephen's Green. Carrying a gas mask had been made mandatory in Britain at the start of the war, and having one to carry would reduce the risk of Elizabeth being stopped and questioned by officialdom.

Also on the Saturday, a letter was posted to the Irish Red Cross Society, asking if they could contact the British authorities to request information about Graham and Ann Shepherd, who were being held in prison in Britain under the Emergency Powers Act. This had been Elizabeth's idea, and it formed an important part of her plan.

A disagreement arose on the Saturday evening when Mike announced that he would accompany Elizabeth on her journey.

"I can't let you do this on your own, Liz, and remain skulking in safety here in Dublin," he said. "At least one of us should travel with you in case a problem arises."

"I know you mean this for the best, Mike," said Elizabeth, "but I must resist this. I've planned this journey to travel alone, and it would complicate things if someone else were to travel with me, as well as the unnecessary risk it would put you in."

As Elizabeth explained her plan in detail, it became clear what she meant. A compromise was eventually reached in which Mike would travel with Elizabeth as far as Larne, where she would board the ferry. One thing Mike did do was to make another quick trip up to Forkhill, travelling as he had done before, in order to post a couple of letters, which formed part of Elizabeth's plan.

On the morning of their departure, Elizabeth and Mike set off from the house and travelled in to the centre of Dublin. Before leaving Dublin, Mike visited his bank and changed £50 into English currency for Elizabeth to use once she reached Britain. At Amiens Street station they boarded a train to Dundalk. Although they were travelling together, they pretended not to know each other, in case either of them was stopped and detained after they had crossed the border. After leaving the train at Dundalk, they walked the short distance from the railway station into the town centre, where they waited in a tea shop until the departure of the next bus for Newry. They sat at different tables, but they both found that the business of ignoring each other was quite difficult. At length, Elizabeth pointedly looked at her watch, got up and left the tea shop, making for the bus station. Half a minute later, Mike did likewise and followed her.

The reason for doing all this was the expectation that it was less likely for there to be checks for identity documents at the border on a local bus service than on the train. And so it proved, at least on this occasion. After leaving Dundalk, the bus wheezed its way along the same road up to Forkhill that Mike had taken on his bicycle. As with many local bus services, it followed a very circuitous route, taking in as many villages as possible. As Mike had found on his bicycle, there were no checks at the border. From Forkhill, the bus made its way through the villages of Drumintee, Meigh and Cloughoge before reaching Newry. At Newry, the bus drove to the town's bus station, which was its route destination. After getting off the bus, Elizabeth and Mike made their way over to where there was a large display board showing timetables for the various bus services out of Newry. They practised the technique of talking while appearing not to be interacting with each other. The next bus to Belfast left in half an hour, so they decided to occupy the time by walking into the town centre and back. After walking for a couple of minutes, Elizabeth came upon a cafe, and decided to go in to have a cup of tea and keep warm, as it was a cold day. Mike, who was following her about thirty yards behind, spotted another cafe further along the street, and decided to go in there to wait. They arrived back at the bus station within a couple of minutes of each other, and boarded the bus to Belfast. The bus was slow, and on this service took the best part of two hours to reach Belfast. From Belfast city centre, they walked the half mile or so along York Street to the Midland Station, the terminus for the line to Larne. Elizabeth walked in front, with Mike following about thirty yards behind her. She walked briskly to keep warm, as the weather was cold and windy. At the ticket office in the station, she bought a train ticket to Larne and a ferry ticket from Larne to Stranraer. Mike, when he reached the counter a couple of minutes later, bought a day return ticket to Larne. There were no complications. On the departure platform, Elizabeth and Mike stood a few yards apart, pretending to ignore each other, which, as before, both of them found quite hard to do. On the train, they sat in adjoining compartments for the forty-minute journey. The train was crowded, mostly with people who were evidently intending to catch the ferry at Larne. Quite a few were in uniform servicemen who were presumably returning to their units on the mainland. Mike found himself sitting next to a sailor who had the ship's name *HMS Witherington* on his hatband.

At Larne, the train stopped at both the town station and the harbour station. Mike stayed on the train until the harbour station, where the service terminated. On the platform at the harbour station, most of the passengers getting off the train made their way to the exit gate for the ferry terminal. For Elizabeth and Mike, this was their moment of parting. It was also the moment when their pretence of ignoring each other finally broke down, and with it, their reserve. In a quiet corner where a line of luggage trolleys screened them from view from the rest of the platform, they stood facing each other.

"I wish you'd let me come with you, Lizzy," Mike said. "I feel awful about letting you go on alone."

"I have to do this on my own, Mike. It isn't just because I've planned it this way, but also because… because of how I'd feel if anything were to happen to you if you came with me."

"Lizzy…"

He reached out and took her into his arms.

"Lizzy, my dearest…"

Her mouth was soft and warm against his as they clung together for long moments, their reserve finally gone.

Seventeen

Elizabeth looked at her watch, having to peer closely at it to read it in the dim lighting of the train compartment. It was just after eight-thirty. According to the timetable, that meant that they should now be running through the outer suburbs of London, although with all the window blinds drawn down because of the blackout regulations it was impossible to see where they were. The drawn blinds induced a sense of claustrophobia as well as making the carriage airless and stuffy because it wasn't possible to open the air vent in the window, and Elizabeth had developed a headache in consequence, as well as being stiff from sitting for hours in the crowded train.

The day had begun that morning in the small hotel in Stranraer, which she had booked into the previous evening, after arriving on the ferry from Larne. The ferry journey had lasted two and a half hours, and had been uneventful beyond the fact that the ferry's departure had been delayed by an hour, apparently because of reports of German U-boats in the Irish Sea. The weather had been fairly calm, so it was a reasonable crossing. On the quayside at Larne, before boarding the ferry, she had been asked for her Identity Card. It was a critical moment, but it passed without incident. She produced her old Identity Card from the Great War, and went through the story about having her handbag stolen. The official had examined the Identity Card intently for several moments, but then just nodded and waved her through. It confirmed that her ruse worked, as well as indicating that she was not on an immediate arrest list, although she would have to wait for confirmation of that.

When the ferry docked at Stranraer, there was no-one waiting for her on the quayside, which, she presumed, there would have been if the authorities were on the lookout for her. From the quayside she made her way into the town. There were three hotels in Stranraer according to Bradshaw's. The George Hotel on George Street had rooms available and she lodged there overnight. At the hotel reception she was again asked for her Identity Card. The receptionist had scrutinised it suspiciously, and seemed to remain suspicious even after she went through the story about having her handbag stolen. The suspicion evaporated when Elizabeth produced her passport; but it had been a tense moment. After an indifferent evening meal in the dining room, she had retired to bed. The room was cold, and the bed not very comfortable, and she had had a restless night in consequence. After a breakfast of tea and toast, she had checked out of the hotel and made her way back to the town railway station. She booked a through ticket to London Euston. She had then wandered into the town and passed the time at a cafe until the train departed. The first part of the journey was to Carlisle via Castle Douglas. The train had been very slow, but the Galloway countryside reminded her of the west of Ireland. At Carlisle there had been a further wait for the next Glasgow to London express, so she took the opportunity to have a quick look at the town centre, as Carlisle wasn't a place she was familiar with. The London express had been ten minutes late, but once aboard the train, Elizabeth had been able to settle down for the long journey. At Warrington, with the daylight fading, the guard went down the train while it was standing in the station, pulling down all the window blinds and warning about the blackout regulations. The rest of the journey was therefore completed in the train's depressingly feeble electric lights. It felt as if they were going through an endless tunnel. When the train finally arrived at Euston, after descending onto the platform, Elizabeth gratefully drank in the cold air to help clear her head.

She went down to Euston Underground station and took the Underground to East Finchley. From East Finchley station she walked up the High Road and turned into Lincoln Road. She had to walk slowly and carefully as all the street lights were turned off. Fortunately, she knew her way. About half-way down Lincoln Road, she knocked at the front door of a tall Victorian semi-detached house. After a minute the door opened, and an anxious face peered out into the darkness.

"Who is it?"

"Bella, it's me, Lizzie."

"Oh, Lizzie, you've arrived," said Bella, and reached out to her. "Come in so I can see you. I can't put the light on because of the blackout."

She drew Elizabeth in and closed the door. After switching the light on, she turned back to Elizabeth.

"Oh, Lizzie, it's so good to see you again. I got your card. It was a bit cryptic, but I guessed what it meant."

Isabella Evans was older than Elizabeth, in her early sixties. Like Elizabeth, she was also a war widow, her husband, a captain in the Royal Engineers, having been killed in the retreat from Mons in 1914. This shared experience had been the basis of a friendship of many years.

"I'm afraid I'm exhausted and absolutely famished, Bella. I've been sitting in crowded trains all day, and I didn't get much sleep last night. I don't know which I need more just now – sleep or food."

"Well, food first, otherwise you'll never eat. I've got some soup I can heat up, and it won't take a few minutes to rustle up another cheese omelette, which is what I had for tea."

"That sounds wonderful!"

***

Elizabeth was too tired to do anything more that night, so it wasn't until the following day that she and Bella were able to talk properly. Over breakfast the following morning, she cautiously explained the reason for her visit.

"It was the thought of the two children which was the main reason why I came. I may not be able to do anything to help Graham and Ann; but if I'm able to help the children in some way, it will bring some relief to them, especially to Ann if she's in prison. I suspect that the children are being held in some kind of institution, which in itself would be enough to make Ann sick with worry."

"How will you find out where the children are?"

"Ann will know. I can't believe they would refuse to tell her where her children are."

"And Ann herself – where is she?"

"We know that she's being held at Holloway prison. We recently asked the Irish Red Cross Society to write to the British Government to ask for information about the whereabouts of Graham and Ann and their two children. They received a reply saying that Graham was being held at Parkhurst prison on the Isle of Wight, and Ann was at Holloway. The children were said to be 'in care', but no details were given."

"How will you get to speak to Ann?"

"I intend to visit her in Holloway prison."

"But... to do that you would have to arrange the visit beforehand, which would mean giving details of your identity. If they knew in advance that you were going to visit, it would give them the perfect opportunity to arrest you."

"If it's what needs to be done, then it's a risk I'm prepared to take. My plan is to write to the Irish Red Cross Society and ask them to arrange my visit. They can then send a private letter to me here to confirm that they've done it, and the time of the visit, if you'll agree to that."

Bella was pensive for a moment.

"If you want me to help you, Lizzie, I feel I can do better than that. First of all, I think it's a very bad idea for you to arrange to visit Holloway prison in that way. There's a high possibility that you'd be walking into a trap, from which you'd never walk out again. Apart from anything else, you'd be able to do nothing to help the children then. If a visit needs to be made to Holloway to speak to Ann, it should be by someone who wouldn't be at such a risk as you would be. I think it would be much more sensible if you let me do this."

"Bella, it wasn't my intention to put you at such risk. I've come here fully intending to take these risks myself."

"But that's precisely my point, Lizzie – if I were to do this, I wouldn't be at the same risk as you. This is one way I could help you."

Elizabeth looked doubtful.

"It would still be a risk, even so," she said.

"Nothing like the risk it would be for you. Particularly if we use the method you've already arranged. If you arrange for the Irish Red Cross Society to notify the authorities that they've designated me as a prison visitor on their behalf, because I'm an ordinary citizen who is willing to do it, then there would be no reason for the authorities to take any action against me unless they were excessively paranoid. Surely you can see that makes sense?"

Elizabeth looked doubtful for a moment, but finally nodded in agreement.

"Yes, I can see that that makes sense. Are you sure you want to do this, Bella?"

"If it will help you find the children, then it's the least I can do. I can imagine only too well how Ann must be feeling."

Elizabeth reached out and touched her arm.

"You share my feelings, then. Thank you."

And so it was arranged. A letter was dispatched to the Irish Red Cross Society that same day to request the necessary arrangements. While they were waiting for the reply, Elizabeth confined herself to the house in order to keep as low a profile as possible. She had experienced a strong temptation to go and see her own house, to see if anything had happened to it; a temptation which she finally resisted. If the house had been left undisturbed, then she would gain little from learning that. If the house had been broken into, by the authorities or anyone else, it would be a distressing discovery she would be able to do nothing about. And it was also possible that the authorities might still be watching the house in case she returned.

Meanwhile, she and Bella caught up with each other's news and, in particular, Elizabeth recounted events since August, when she had gone to Ireland. Bella knew about National Renaissance, and while not a member of the group, was generally sympathetic. Not being greatly interested in politics, she had not been motivated to join the group. Listening to Elizabeth's narrative of events since August, however, caused her to feel a sense of disquiet.

"It strikes a rather different note from what we hear on the wireless or read in the newspapers," she said. "War has a dark side; but one doesn't associate this kind of thing with England – at least not so that we're led to believe."

159

"Most people never question what they're told, and so have no occasion to think such thoughts," said Elizabeth. "It's only those who do ask questions who find out, particularly at a time such as this, that doing so can be dangerous. It's all very well citing a need for national security in such cases, but when a government is immunised from all criticism by such measures, it becomes prone to taking some very bad decisions."

"National security is a sort of catch all for just about everything now. I suppose that's inevitable at a time of war; but such a drastic response to public criticism still seems un-English somehow, even in wartime."

"But we were not at war when they came to arrest us – when they arrested Graham and Ann. They didn't even wait to give us the benefit of the doubt. I know that those of us in our group who had to flee are still patriotic. We would never betray our country by working for the enemy in wartime. And from the things we had written and published, there was no reason to think that we would."

"It feels very unsettling to know that such things could happen here. You were always more interested in politics than I was, Lizzie, perhaps because you were aware of these things; and I'm still not sure I can take all this in. But what I feel most strongly about is what's happened to the children. I'm ready to do whatever I can to help."

"I'm very grateful for that, Bella, but I don't want to expose you to risks unnecessarily. The best way you can help is to gather information. As far as possible, it should be me who takes any risks. I came back to England prepared to do that. If you can find out from Ann what happened when they were arrested, and what happened to the children, you can do me no greater service."

By the time the letter of reply from the Irish Red Cross Society arrived, confirming the arrangement for Bella to act as their representative, Bella's visit to Ann had been discussed and planned in detail, to prepare for as many eventualities as possible. When the letter arrived, it confirmed that Bella had been nominated as a prison visitor on behalf of the Society to visit Ann Shepherd at Holloway prison, where she was being detained without trial on a political charge. With the letter was a document which Bella was to take with her, confirming that she was acting on behalf of the Society. Bella immediately wrote to the governor of the prison, requesting that a visit be arranged. Three days later, a letter of reply was received. It confirmed the visit, and set a date and time for it, four days hence.

The waiting that this process inevitably involved told more on Elizabeth than on Bella, who, outwardly at least, remained very calm. They passed some of the time playing board games such as chequers or Monopoly; but mostly they had long discussions about a wide range of subjects from science to ancient history, as well as personal reminiscences about their husbands and children. Bella had two children: a son in his late thirties, who worked for an engineering company in the Midlands; and a daughter in her early thirties who lived nearby.

On the day of the prison visit, both of them were rather tense with nerves. The appointment to visit the prison was at ten-thirty in the morning. Holloway prison was not far from where Bella lived: three stops down on the Underground from East Finchley station, and then a fifteen-minute walk. Bella set off from the house at nine-thirty to give herself plenty of time. Before she left, Elizabeth went through with her the questions she needed to ask Ann, and things she needed to look out for, and what to do in different eventualities. After a final "Good luck" from Elizabeth, Bella set off into the rather dank December morning. For Elizabeth there was then a long and anxious wait. Midday came and went with no sign of Bella, and by two o'clock she had a feeling of certainty that the worst had happened. She didn't move from where she sat in Bella's lounge, oppressed by thoughts of self-condemnation and uncertainty about what she was going to do. She decided that if Bella didn't return soon, she would have to assume that Bella had been arrested, and that she would have to try to contact Bella's daughter, Jane. This was what Bella had suggested in such an eventuality. Jane would be in a position to go to the prison to try to see her mother. It would mean searching in Bella's address book to find Jane's address, which Elizabeth didn't know. At length, she could wait no longer. She went and got her coat. She found Jane's address in the book. Jane lived in Harrow – to get there would mean taking the Underground in to Euston, then out again to Harrow. It was already mid-afternoon, and there wasn't much daylight left. She checked her purse to see how much money she had left. At that moment she heard the sound of a key in the front door. She went out into the hall. It was Bella.

"Bella! Oh, Bella, I thought you were lost. I assumed the worst must have happened and you'd been arrested. I was about to set off to go and see Jane."

"Lizzie, I'm so sorry. I'm afraid I've tried to do too much, and I lost track of time. I should have thought more about how you'd worry, so I'm so sorry, Lizzie."

"I'm just so glad to see you back, Bella. I couldn't have forgiven myself if anything had happened to you. Did you manage to see Ann?"

Bella nodded, her face becoming serious as she did so.

"Yes. Yes, I did. I've so much to tell you." Her face twisted suddenly. "But… Oh, Lizzie. Lizzie – you've been betrayed!"

Eighteen

They had settled in Bella's lounge after a hastily arranged meal, which was consumed with equal haste as both of them had been famished. Neither of them spoke much during the meal, being too busy eating, so it wasn't until they had settled in the lounge that Bella was able to begin her account of what had happened.

"I suppose the most nerve-racking part of it was when I was approaching the prison entrance, about to go in," she said. "Never having done anything like this before, I wasn't sure what to expect; but I assumed that if I was going to run into a problem, I would know about it fairly quickly. When I arrived, I had to wait with a small group of other people for the gate to be opened. We were taken over to a guardhouse, where each of us was seen in turn by a prison officer. I had to explain who I was, what the purpose of my visit was, and produce the official permit to visit. I was then searched by a female prison officer, and although she searched my bag, she only gave my purse a perfunctory inspection. This was the point where I expected to find out if I had walked into a trap; but nothing seemed to happen. We then all had to wait in a waiting room. We were called for in small groups at a time, at intervals of about twenty minutes. We were taken across a yard to another building, escorted by two prison officers. Every door we went through was unlocked and then locked again after we'd gone through.

"The visiting room was divided down the middle by a partition with several windows in it. The prisoner sat on one side of the window, the visitor on the other. I was told to go and sit at window number four. A minute or two later, a prison officer escorted a woman to the seat on the other side of the window. I've met Ann before, of course; but at first I didn't recognise her. For a moment I thought they'd made a mistake and sent the wrong prisoner to the window. But Ann recognised me, and I saw that of course it was Ann. But they'd cut her hair very short, almost like a man's, and it seemed to change her. It was as if they'd done it to humiliate her. I noticed that all the women prisoners had had their hair cut in the same way. I felt shocked when I saw this.

"Oh, she was so pleased to see me, Lizzie. I could see the emotion in her face, and it moved me to tears. I can only imagine what she must have been going through. I explained that I'd been contacted by the Irish Red Cross Society in Dublin who had asked me to visit her, because they'd received information from friends of hers that she'd been arrested and was being held without trial. I mentioned that her friends were now in Dublin. She understood what I meant.

"I had to be careful about what I did next, as there was a prison officer standing at the back of the room behind Ann, and another at the opposite end of the room behind me. I opened my purse and slid the bit of paper from out of the lining and opened it out, holding the purse just high enough for Ann to read what was written on it without either of the guards being able to see it.

"Ann read it, and was thoughtful for a moment. She looked a little puzzled, and then said that no-one had come to warn them at any time about the danger they were in of being arrested, and that the first thing they knew about it was when the police had turned up on the morning of their arrest. There was no warning. It wasn't the answer I was expecting. The question written on the paper assumed that they had received the warning. I had to think quickly about what to say, so I just said: 'You didn't receive any warning?' Ann just shook her head and continued to look puzzled. I understood the truth in that moment, about what must have happened; but I didn't dare say any more. The speaking grille set into the partition certainly could have contained a microphone.

"When I asked her about her children, and whether she had had any contact with them, her face again twisted with emotion. She said that being separated from her children and knowing that they, too, were in distress was the hardest thing for her to bear. She had only received two letters, one from each of the children, since the arrest.

However, she said that the wording of the letter from Susan suggested that other letters had been sent which Ann had never received. She said that both letters were very constrained, indicating that the children had not been free to write as they might have wished; but that their unhappiness and distress could not be concealed, even then.

"When I asked her where the children were, she said they were being held at a local authority children's home at Epping in Essex. She gave me the address. By this point, time was running short, so I said that I would include the information about the children in my report to the Irish Red Cross Society, and ask if anything might be done for them. We would do whatever we could to help. I said I would visit her again as soon as that could be arranged through the Society, and we would also try to arrange a visit to Graham. This seemed to give her some comfort; but I found it very distressing to have to leave her in that place.

"When I left the prison it was still only lunchtime and, as I felt emboldened by the fact that things had gone so well, I made an impulsive decision. Now that I knew where the children were, and given that it was only in Epping, I decided to go and have a look at the place straight away. I took the Underground to Liverpool Street, from where I could get a train out to Epping. There was a bit of a wait at Liverpool Street for a connecting train, so it was well after one o'clock by the time I got to Epping. Epping's only a small town, so it didn't take long to find the children's home. It's in a large, detached house in its own grounds, half a mile or so from the station. I walked down a side road running alongside the house, and although the property is surrounded by railings, I could look through them into the back garden or yard, which appears to be a children's play area. The yard appeared to be divided down the middle by a solid wooden fence, about five feet high. There were no children visible at the time.

"After having a good look round the outside of the place from the street, I walked back to the station. I was buoyed up by having achieved more than I'd hoped for, and still not thinking how you must have been worried by my non-appearance. It was only when I got back to the station that I realised how late it was, and that you'd be wondering what had happened, so I am sorry, Lizzie."

"No, you've done extraordinarily well, Bella. You've achieved everything that might have been hoped for today, and more, so thank you."

Bella nodded and smiled; but after a moment, her face became serious again.

"But… Duncan Watkinson…"

Elizabeth shook her head slowly.

"It's hard for me to take in, Bella. But no other conclusion is possible. Bob Aldcroft went to see Duncan Watkinson on the day he warned everyone about the impending arrests, and Duncan told him he would drive out to warn Graham and Ann that evening. When Mike Warren spoke to Duncan on the telephone from Ireland some time later, Duncan told him that he'd driven out to Ridgewell and warned Graham and Ann about the impending arrest. It's now clear that he didn't. The only explanation is that he betrayed us – and always intended to betray us. I never thought that such a thing could happen in our little group."

"What will you do, now that you know?"

Elizabeth was silent for a moment.

"In other circumstances, I might have gone to confront Duncan Watkinson about his betrayal. But that isn't the reason why I've returned to England. My priority has to be the children. Also, perhaps it wouldn't be appropriate for me to decide the matter on my own. I'll explain what I've discovered to the group, and we will decide together what will be the best thing to do – assuming I make it back to Dublin."

Nineteen

As soon as they had eaten, Bella began drafting her report of the visit for the Irish Red Cross Society. Time was now of the essence. By the late evening, she had finished the draft, consulting with Elizabeth over various points of information. The following morning, she read through the draft again, made one or two minor corrections, and then began typing out the report, with a carbon copy, on an old typewriter she had. By midday the finished report, with a brief covering letter, was enveloped and addressed, and having been taken to the local post office, was on its way to Dublin.

Elizabeth decided that she would use that afternoon to have a quick look at the children's home herself. After some discussion, it was decided that Bella would go with her, so that she would know if anything untoward happened; but they would pretend not to know each other, for the benefit of anyone who might be watching them. After a quick lunch, they made their way separately to the Underground station. Making the trip was an additional risk for Elizabeth of being stopped and questioned by the authorities; but she judged that it was a risk worth taking in this instance. And so it proved to be.

At Epping, they left the station separately, with Bella leading the way. The children's home was ten minutes' or so walk from the station. Bella indicated the place to Elizabeth by stopping at the entrance for a few moments and looking back at Elizabeth briefly, before continuing on down the street. As it happened, there was a bus stop about 150 yards or so down the street, where Bella stopped and waited. After a few minutes, Elizabeth joined her, apparently also waiting for a bus.

"I'm going to loiter for a while to see if I can see anything interesting or useful," Elizabeth said. "Will you loiter with me? Two pairs of eyes are better than one."

Bella thought for a moment, then shook her head.

"Two people hanging about suspiciously is too risky. There's a good chance someone might call the police, especially at the present time." She smiled for a moment. "German spies?" she said.

"I suppose you're right."

"How long do you need?"

"An hour, say?"

"I'll tell you what, then. I'll walk into the town centre and find a tea shop on the High Street, and I'll meet you back at the station in –" she looked at her watch "– an hour and a quarter."

Elizabeth looked at her watch.

"Right – an hour and a quarter at the station. See you then!"

Bella set off down the road back towards the town centre. Elizabeth remained standing at the bus stop for a few minutes until Bella was out of sight, before slowly starting to walk back towards the children's home. She had no definite plan in mind, other than to get an idea of the layout of the place, and to see if she could spot anything of interest.

The children's home was a large, three-storeyed, detached Victorian villa, built of dark red brick, much extended at the back, and with multiple dormer windows in the roof. As Bella had described, the property was surrounded by railings about six feet high, which meant that she had a good view of it from the street. On her first perambulation around the place, there was little sign of activity, other than what she assumed to be the janitor emptying rubbish into dustbins at the side of the house. Gates and fencing separated the grounds at the front of the building from the grounds at the back. The grounds at the back appeared to be a children's play area. This was divided down the middle by a wooden fence about five feet high, presumably for the purpose of separating the boys from the girls.

This last was confirmed on Elizabeth's next perambulation. Even as she approached, having walked back from the town centre, she heard the noise of children playing. When she arrived, she saw that the children had been released into the area at the back of the building, confirming it was a children's play area. The children on the side of the wooden partition that she could see, next to the railings, were the girls. As she scanned the playground, she suddenly saw Susan Shepherd. She experienced a sudden surge of emotion, and almost before she had time to think, she called out: "Susan!"

Several girls looked round in response; but one of them was Susan Shepherd. There was surprise and hope in her expression as she recognised Elizabeth. She came over to where Elizabeth was standing by the railings.

"Mrs Lacey! It's Mrs Lacey, isn't it?"

"Hello, Susan."

Elizabeth indicated that they should move along a few yards to be out of earshot of the other children.

"I can only stay here for a minute or two," she continued. "I went to Ireland, to Dublin, just before the war started, because we received a warning that we were going to be arrested. We're safe in Dublin. The same warning was supposed to go to your mum and dad, but they were betrayed, which is why they were arrested. The Irish Red Cross Society has visited your mum where she's being held, and she told them where you and Richard are. Are you able to speak to Richard?"

"Yes. We're kept separate from the boys, but I can speak to him through the fence." She pointed to the wooden fence dividing the play area.

"Make sure no-one else is listening when you speak to him. Would you like to come back to Dublin with me? Most of our group are there now, including George and Christine Harvey and little Barbara and Angela. We're all living in a big house there owned by Mike Warren."

"Oh, I'd love to, and so would Richard, I know. But they won't let us out of here. They've told us that."

"You'd have to escape. Do you think you'd be able to do that?"

Susan thought for a moment.

"We're locked in when we're inside. But I could get out through a toilet window. But I'd still have to get over this." She indicated the railings that separated them.

"Don't worry, I'd help you from this side. Do they let you out to play here at the same time every day?"

Susan nodded.

"It will probably be the day after tomorrow," said Elizabeth. "When you see me here again during playtime, you will know that it will be that evening. What time do you normally finish tea, or evening meal?"

"About half-past five; then we have to go to the dorms."

"Make your escape as soon as you can after you've finished tea. It's important that Richard makes his escape at the same time, so make sure you explain the plan to him clearly. But don't let anyone else hear you. Do you think Richard will be able to get over that fence?"

"Yes, he will. He's climbed over it before, to come and see if I'm alright. He told me afterwards he got beaten for it as punishment."

"Well, I'm going to get you both out of this place. Now, do you think you can remember everything? When you next see me during afternoon playtime, you'll know it's going to be that evening; so as soon after tea as you can that evening, make your escape. When you see me during playtime, don't wave to me or anything, but come up to the railings and look in my direction, so I know that you've seen me. It's probably going to be the day after tomorrow. When you've escaped from the house, come over to the railings here and I'll be waiting for you. I'll help you to climb over. Keep watch each afternoon playtime, but as I say, it's probably going to be the day after tomorrow. I have to make preparations to ensure we can get away safely to Dublin. Now – I want you to point down the street as though you were pointing something out to me."

Looking a little puzzled, Susan did so.

"If anyone asks you why you were talking to me, just say I was a stranger who was passing by who was asking for directions to the town centre. Don't tell them you know me – say I was a stranger. Say you couldn't help me much, as you don't really know this place. Now, do you think you can remember everything?"

Susan nodded and smiled.

"You'll soon be out of here, and free in Ireland," Elizabeth said. She reached through the railings and gently squeezed the child's hand. Susan smiled again; but it was Elizabeth who was most affected by that momentary contact, reaching out for the first time to one of the children she had made this uncertain journey to rescue.

A quarter of an hour later, Elizabeth was back at the station. Bella was already in the waiting room when she arrived, sitting reading a book. They didn't openly acknowledge each other, but when Elizabeth sat down, she glanced at Bella and gave a discreet thumbs-up sign to indicate that things had gone well.

Back at Bella's house they began preparations for a more leisurely evening meal, over which there was an animated discussion of the day's events. Bella was enthusiastic about how well things had gone that day; but neither of them was under any illusion about the difficulties that lay ahead.

"Not many would have the fortitude to do what you are doing," said Bella. "I greatly admire you for it."

But Elizabeth shook her head.

"It's no longer a matter of choice, Bella. When I touched that child's hand this afternoon and saw the look of hope in her eyes, there's nothing I wouldn't do to justify the trust she has in me to get them out of that place and to freedom. If I do nothing else in my life, I will do this if it's humanly possible."

Twenty

That evening was the beginning of what seemed like an interminable wait, which lasted throughout the following day. There were things to be done, however, in preparation for the escape attempt. In the morning, Elizabeth went to a clothing shop on the local high street and bought two children's coats and two woolly hats. As well as giving the children a measure of disguise, it would ensure that they had warm coats. The weather was starting to turn very cold, with the promise of even colder weather to come. She also went to the local library and spent some time making notes from the latest edition of Bradshaw's railway timetable. She purchased some items from a hardware store, including a torch, a vacuum flask and a small compass.

Bella spent much of the day producing a number of items to assist in giving the two children false identities. It was decided that whilst they were travelling, the children would pretend to be Elizabeth's children, using the names Stephen and Jennifer Lacey. The fact that Elizabeth had a real daughter called Jennifer would, it was hoped, lend credibility to the deception. Since the real Jennifer was in Canada, it would be difficult for the authorities to sort out the truth from fiction.

Back at Bella's house, Elizabeth repacked the small suitcase she had brought with her, taking out items to make room for some of the things she had bought. They talked long into the evening, whilst preparing the evening meal, and long after the meal itself. The main outcome of their discussions was to agree the best courses of action for Bella in the event that the rescue attempt went wrong or failed, and Elizabeth and the children ended up being taken by the authorities.

"I've become completely involved in this," said Bella. "It's a marvellous thing to do, to rescue the children like this. I do wish you'd let me come with you, Lizzie, at least as far as the ferry to Ireland. It's going to be a long and difficult wait, not knowing whether you've succeeded, or what may have happened to you."

"It would be a comfort to me if you did, Bella, as it's going to be difficult to do this on my own. But it's just as important to me that nothing should happen to you because of this, and that must include not taking any unnecessary risks. Coming with me would be an unnecessary risk because if anything were to happen, there's nothing you'd be able to do, and if you tried to intervene, you'd only end up being taken yourself. I couldn't forgive myself if that were to happen." She reached out and touched her friend's hand. "What you've done already is by far the most effective way you could have helped me. Without the help that you've given me, especially the risk you took in going to Holloway, I wouldn't have been able to do this. If anything does go wrong, it will also be a comfort to me to know that you will be here, not only safe, but also in the best position to be able to help if that were possible. It will be a hard wait, I know, Bella, but whatever happens, I will get a message to you somehow to let you know. I promise!"

That night, Elizabeth didn't get much sleep, even though she knew it was important that she should do. As she lay awake, she thought about her own daughter, Jennifer, at much the same age that Susan was now, and tried to imagine how she would feel if Jennifer were in the same situation, and she, Elizabeth, was, like Ann, powerless to help her child. Such thoughts were not a good place to go, even in imagination.

Both Bella and Elizabeth were up early the following morning. Neither felt much like eating breakfast. This was the hardest part of the wait. But their emotions were transformed when, at just after ten o'clock, there was a ring at the doorbell. It was a messenger from the Post Office, with a telegram for Bella. It was from the Irish Red Cross Society in Dublin, and it read simply: 'Your letter received with thanks.' Bella and Elizabeth looked at each other. Words were insufficient, and they simply hugged each other with emotion. The change of mood affected them both, but especially Elizabeth. Now that Bella's cover was confirmed, she could look forward to the day's events, and all their difficulties, with a renewed confidence.

Final preparations for Elizabeth's departure took them up to lunchtime. Both of them had a much better appetite for lunch than they had had for breakfast. Elizabeth ate a substantial lunch, to keep her going for as long as possible. Bella also made some sandwiches, which Elizabeth was able to squeeze into her suitcase.

They stood and faced each other as Elizabeth was about to depart.

"It's going to be hard, waiting and not knowing."

"I can never repay you enough for all your help, Bella. Whatever happens, I will get a message to you to let you know. And if I succeed, I'd like you to come and visit us in Dublin. It will be wonderful to see you again!"

From East Finchley, Elizabeth took the Underground down to Euston. At Euston train station, she bought one adult and two children's tickets to Glasgow. It was something of a risk buying the tickets at this point; but it would be a greater risk buying the tickets once the children were with her. From Euston she took the Underground to Liverpool Street for the connection to Epping. She arrived in Epping shortly after half-past two. Leaving the station, she noticed how cold the weather had become. There were one or two flakes of snow in the air.

By three o'clock she was in the vicinity of the children's home. When she first walked past, there was no sign of any activity, so she walked slowly round the block. On her second approach she heard the sound of children playing in the playground. Before walking past the playground, she crossed to the other side of the street. She slowed as she came level with the playground, finally coming to a stop, facing it from across the street. It was a minute before she saw Susan, who had already seen her. Susan came up to the railings, and stood looking at Elizabeth, and smiling. Elizabeth smiled back, and nodded significantly, to indicate that the escape was on. She began walking again, looking back once and smiling again at Susan, who watched until she was out of sight.

From the children's home, Elizabeth walked back into the town centre. She went to the local library to spend the two hours or so she needed to wait. Whilst there, she looked through some of the directories in the reference section, noting down bits of information she thought might be useful. At five o'clock she left the town centre, and by twenty-past five she was again in the street alongside the children's home. She walked slowly alongside the railings, staring into the darkened playground for some sign of the children. As well as being very dark, it was also now very chilly. By 5.35, she was starting to become worried, having seen no sign of the children. Then she heard some muffled sounds from within the playground. There was the sound of whispering, and then she heard Susan calling in a loud whisper:

"Mrs Lacey. Are you there?"

"Yes, I'm here, Susan. Is Richard with you?"

"Yes, I'm here," Richard whispered.

"Is everything alright?"

"Yes, we both managed to sneak out through toilet windows," whispered Richard.

"Right," said Elizabeth, "Susan first. Stand against the railings."

Susan did so. Elizabeth reached through the railings and lifted Susan up until she could scramble onto the top of the railings. Elizabeth then lifted her down to the ground on the pavement beside her.

"Now Richard."

Richard was a lot heavier than Susan, and Elizabeth struggled to lift him.

"Susan, can you help?"

Susan reached through and pushed her brother up from below as best she could. Between the two of them they managed to lift Richard high enough for him to scramble onto the top of the railings, from where Elizabeth then lifted him down.

"Right, quickly now!"

It was important to get away from the children's home as quickly as possible. They walked briskly back to the town centre, stopping once on the way so that the children could don the coats and hats Elizabeth had brought. As they approached the station, Elizabeth explained the procedure she wanted to follow for getting tickets and boarding the train.

Elizabeth approached the entrance into the station from one side, keeping the children behind her. She moved forward slowly, looking casually into the entrance. There was no sign of the police or anything unusual, so she motioned to the children to wait where they were, just out of sight. She went up to the ticket counter and bought one adult and two children's tickets to Liverpool Street station.

Back with the children, she gave Richard his ticket, keeping the other two. Richard then went by himself through the ticket barrier and out onto the platform, walking along to the footbridge to cross over to the platform for London-bound trains. A minute or so later Elizabeth and Susan followed him. The procedure was that Richard would pretend that he was travelling alone, and had nothing to do with Elizabeth and Susan.

When the next train arrived, Richard boarded it first. Elizabeth and Susan boarded the same carriage, but through the door at the other end. They moved along the carriage and sat a few seats away from where Richard had taken his seat. At Liverpool Street, they went down to the Underground station, with Richard following Elizabeth and Susan, about ten yards behind. Elizabeth bought tickets for the three of them for Euston Square, and discreetly slipped Richard his ticket. Elizabeth and Susan went down to the platform, again with Richard following. They all boarded the same carriage, and Richard sat a few seats away from the other two. As they approached Euston Square, Elizabeth caught Richard's eye to indicate that theirs was the next stop. At Euston Square, they briefly stood together on the platform while Elizabeth explained the street directions to Richard, so that he could take the lead. On reaching the street entrance on Gower Street, Richard turned right and walked up to the first road junction, with Euston Road. He stopped and waited, looking out for the traffic. The other two caught up with him and waited also. One or two other pedestrians joined them. They all crossed together, and on the far side, Richard strode out ahead to open up a short distance between himself and the other two. The same procedure was repeated at each road junction until they had crossed Drummond Street. Elizabeth and Susan now walked ahead, with Richard following a short distance behind. Elizabeth led the way to the station entrance.

In the great hall, Elizabeth led the way over to where there were several public telephone booths, and indicated that Richard should sit on a seat a few feet away. She went into one of the booths, taking Susan in with her. She put a call through to the Station Hotel in Carlisle and booked a family room for that night. She advised that she would be arriving late, but was told that there would be a night porter on duty.

Time was now tight if they were to catch the evening mail train to Glasgow. After checking the arrivals and departures board, Elizabeth gave Richard his train ticket, telling him to go on ahead and make his way to the platform for the Glasgow train. She and Susan followed a short distance behind him. At the ticket barrier, Richard went through and out onto the platform. Elizabeth and Susan followed. After walking along the length of the train for some distance, Richard stopped at a particular carriage and looked back. Elizabeth nodded, and Richard boarded the carriage. Elizabeth and Susan boarded the same carriage by the door at the other end. They then had to walk along the corridor to see which compartment Richard was in. Richard had found an empty compartment and taken a seat by the window, although the window blind was already drawn down because of the blackout regulations.

"Remember to keep pretending that we don't know each other," Elizabeth told him quickly. "We'll be getting off at Carlisle – that's part of my plan."

After a minute, two or three other people came into the compartment, preventing further conversation. Elizabeth and Susan sat by the compartment door. Elizabeth was able to relax a little once the train started moving. As with most of her journey down to London, the journey north was stuffy and claustrophobic with all the window blinds down.

For the children, the journey was still something of an adventure. Normally by this time, they would be confined to their dormitories for the night; instead, they were now roaring northwards through the night on an express train towards a hoped-for freedom. For Elizabeth, the journey was only an interlude until the next point of danger.

The guard came into the compartment to check tickets. Elizabeth was apprehensive for a moment in case he also asked to see identity documents; but he didn't. As he left the compartment he announced where the train would stop next, which was Rugby. This happened after each station where the train stopped, the last one before Carlisle being Penrith. Elizabeth waited until the train began to slow as it approached Carlisle. One other person in the compartment got up, obviously intending to get out at Carlisle. Elizabeth also got up, glancing quickly at Richard and giving him a slight nod. Richard followed Elizabeth and Susan into the corridor. The train lurched slowly over points and swung to the left as it approached the platform, coming to a halt in a squeal of brakes. Out on the platform, the three of them stood together for a moment. Elizabeth said to Richard:

"You walk in front as before. Over the footbridge, then once you're through the ticket barrier, wait for us just outside the station entrance."

Richard set off in front of them. As Elizabeth had noted previously, at Carlisle, tickets were not checked for passengers leaving the station. Walking over the footbridge, she looked down at the ticket barrier and saw that that still appeared to be the case. There was no sign of the police. Once through the barrier, she asked Susan to go over to a rack holding various printed leaflets in the entrance hall and pretend to look through it, while Elizabeth went into the ticket office. In the ticket office, Elizabeth bought one adult and two children's rail tickets to Stranraer, and one adult and two children's ferry tickets across to Larne. Back in the entrance hall she went over to Susan, and they went out to where Richard was waiting for them.

Outside, it was noticeably colder than in London, and there was continuous light snow falling, although it wasn't settling much yet. The station entrance faced onto a square, with the station building forming its southwest side. The southeast side of the square was formed by the Station Hotel, the entrance of which was dimly visible. Inside, the hotel lobby was deserted, so Elizabeth rang the bell for the night porter, who appeared a minute later. He looked in the hotel register and confirmed the telephone booking she had made. As she had expected, he asked her for her National Identity Card. She produced her passport and her old Identity Card, and went through the story about having had her handbag stolen. She then produced the documents which Bella had created for the children, explaining that, as the children were at boarding school, they hadn't yet been issued with National Identity Cards. The man seemed satisfied with this and signed them in to the register with no further comment. He unlocked a key cabinet behind the counter and took out one of the keys on the rack.

"Room twelve. It's up the stairs, turn right at the top, then along the corridor. The bathroom and toilet are at the end of the corridor. Remember to keep all curtains and blinds drawn until daylight. Breakfast is at eight o'clock."

Elizabeth thanked him, and bade him goodnight. She led the children up the stairs and along to room twelve. The room was not particularly large, but it contained a double bed, two single beds, a cot for a small child, an armchair, a small table and a wardrobe. It was cold. Elizabeth turned the radiator on, but it didn't seem to make much difference. The children were now hungry, so Elizabeth brought out the sandwiches Bella had made, and a packet of biscuits and a bottle of lemonade which she had bought in Epping.

After settling the children down to sleep, Elizabeth wrote a short note to Bella, letting her know that they had got as far as Carlisle, before retiring to bed herself. When she eventually got off to sleep, it was after midnight; and when she awoke it was already twenty-to-eight. She quickly woke the children and told them to get dressed and ready. She peeped round the curtain to find that dawn was now breaking. Their room was on the first floor of the hotel at the front, and the window looked out over the station square. It had continued to snow during the night and the cobbles of the square were now hidden by a thin covering of snow, which brightened and intensified the dim, grey dawn light. On the other side of the square, facing the hotel, was one of the red-brown sandstone round towers of the old city gates. She quickly got dressed and ready herself, rounded up the children and took them downstairs to the hotel dining room. Breakfast was necessarily hurried if they were to catch the Stranraer train, but she urged the children to eat as much as they could, nevertheless. During the meal she made a point of calling them by their assumed names of Stephen and Jennifer, both to remind them of the names, and for the benefit of anyone listening. By twenty-to nine they were back upstairs in room twelve, packing their belongings into Elizabeth's suitcase and donning coats and hats. Downstairs in the lobby, Elizabeth paid the bill and handed in the key. She then told the children to wait in the lobby while she went across to the station. Outside, it was still snowing – still only light snow, but it was settling. The sky was leaden with snow clouds. She went into the station entrance, looking about for any indication that there might be a problem. But there was no sign of the police, or that anything else was amiss. She checked the departure board, and returned to the hotel. She gave Richard his train ticket so that he could go through first, telling him to wait on the far platform, over the footbridge. Shortly afterwards, she and Susan followed. There was no problem at the ticket barrier. Before crossing the footbridge, Elizabeth dropped her letter to Bella into the station post box, and a minute later, they joined the other passengers on the far platform who were waiting for the Stranraer train. They stood near enough to Richard to ensure that they would all be able to board the same carriage. As before, Elizabeth and Susan walked along the corridor of the carriage until they found Richard's compartment, and took seats at the opposite end of the compartment. Elizabeth's last glimpse of Carlisle was of the dark red-brown sandstone of the castle walls standing above brilliant white fields of snow.

The entire landscape was now white, as the train made its way slowly through the empty Galloway countryside, stopping at each small town along the way: Dumfries, Castle Douglas, Newton Stewart. Just beyond Glenluce there was a first glimpse of the sea, in Luce Bay.

At Stranraer, the train ran straight out to the harbour station at the end of the long jetty. On leaving the train, they stood together on the station platform. They would certainly be asked for identity documents before boarding the steamer, so this time they had to stay together. First, led by Elizabeth, they made their way along the platform to its northernmost end. Beyond the end of the station building, there were railings, through which it was possible to see the harbour basin, where the steamer was tied up alongside the quay. The gangways from the quayside were up against the ship's side, and people were already boarding the ship. There was no sign of the police on the quayside, or any indication of unusual activity there, so Elizabeth led the way back down the platform towards the ticket barrier. On the way, she posted another note to Bella in the station letter box, letting Bella know that they had made it as far as Stranraer.

There was no sign of the police at the ticket barrier, but as expected, they were asked for identity documents. Watching the queue in front of her, Elizabeth noted that the official was having to cope with people who didn't have their National Identity Card with them and were having to provide some other form of identification. When it was her turn, she produced her passport and old Identity Card, and went through the stories about her handbag being stolen, and her children being at boarding school. The official looked at the documents, nodded without comment, and indicated they should pass through. Evidently, Elizabeth's name was not yet on a 'wanted' list, so the official was content to let her pass. There was a long queue behind her.

Out on the quayside, a railway company clerk checked their steamer tickets, and they then walked up the gangway and onto the ship. They made their way to the main passenger lounge and found seats there. For Elizabeth, it was a rather tense wait, and the children also became restless. The ship wasn't due to sail until one-thirty, more than an hour hence; but the ship's cafeteria would not open until after the ship sailed. Richard asked if he could go and explore the ship. At first, Elizabeth was against the idea; but given that the children, Richard in particular, continued to be unsettled, she relented, and they all set off to explore. In fact, because the cafeteria was still closed, a lot of people were moving around the decks of the ship, not yet settled. They went up and down various companion ways to visit all the decks that were open to passengers. Out on the open top deck, and on the poop deck, the children played hide and seek around air vents and under lifeboats. From the top deck there were good views of the harbour and the bay, which formed the southern end of Loch Ryan. Eventually, even the children began to feel the cold, and they retreated back to the warmth of the main passenger lounge. Light snow was continuing to fall, and was beginning to settle on the ship's decks and upper works. From the passenger lounge, they watched as the gangways were pulled away and the mooring ropes untied as the ship made ready to sail. The ship trembled as the engines began to turn the propellers, and the ship went slowly astern as it pulled away from the jetty. Once well clear of the jetty, it began to turn until the bow was pointing towards the mouth of the loch. The ship trembled again as the propellers were reversed, and they began to make headway towards the mouth of the loch.

As the cafeteria was now open, they went to get a meal while the ship was still in the relatively calm waters of Loch Ryan. In fact, once clear of the loch, the ship encountered only a moderate sea state, as the wind was fairly light. It continued to snow, however, with the snow seeming to get heavier as they approached the Irish coast. Dusk was approaching as the ship edged into Larne harbour.

They remained in the main passenger lounge as the ship was tied up alongside the quay. It was as well they did so, because, looking through the window out onto the quayside, Elizabeth saw the first sign of trouble. There were several police officers on the quayside, some of them conferring with railway company officials. The gangways were run up to the ship's side and, at each one, a police officer stood alongside the railway company official. This was clearly out of the ordinary, and Elizabeth was in no doubt what it was about. Richard and Susan's absence from the children's home would have been discovered by that morning at the latest. When it was discovered that both of them – brother and sister – were missing, it would be obvious that they had escaped together. Once the police had been notified, at the very least, a general alert would be put out to railway stations and ports to watch for the two children. That had clearly now happened, evidently while the ship had been crossing the North Channel. Beyond that, it was also possible that an alert had been put out for Elizabeth herself. When Susan had called out: "Mrs Lacey!" in the playground, had any of the other children heard? Had the name registered? It seemed prudent to assume that they were also now looking for her.

As she watched, she saw that the police officers were looking specifically at any children who were disembarking, which left the matter in no doubt. She had to think quickly about what they were going to do. She turned to the children and said: "I'm afraid we've got a problem. Come with me."

She led them out of the passenger lounge and out onto the upper deck. Richard had also noticed the police and understood what she meant. From the upper deck there was a good view of the ship and the quayside. Elizabeth told the children to stay back out of sight while she went up to the rail to take in the details of the scene. She didn't notice Richard, keeping low, sneaking up to the rail and hiding underneath one of the lifeboats, from where he cast a schoolboy's eye over the scene. As Elizabeth watched, people continued to disembark along the gangways; but she knew that it wouldn't be long before the last passengers left. It was likely that the crew would then check all the passenger areas to make sure that there were no passengers left on board. Elizabeth walked back to where Susan was waiting.

"Where's... ?" she began to say, and Susan pointed. Elizabeth turned round as Richard emerged from beneath the lifeboat and came over. Elizabeth sighed, but she then said quietly: "The police are looking for you two. That's what they're doing here on the quayside. It's obvious that an alert has now been put out. They may well also be looking for me, so all three of us are now in danger. We need to find somewhere to hide here on the ship, perhaps for an hour or so, until things have quietened down and they think all the passengers have left. We can't hide in any of the passenger cabins because the crew will search those, so it will have to be somewhere on deck."

"I know the perfect place," said Richard. "It's right near the stern of the ship. I found it when we were exploring the ship when we first came on board."

"Right, well we'll stay together," said Elizabeth.

They went down onto the poop deck, keeping to the port side, which was the side away from the quay. There were still a few passengers on the poop deck, but they were now making their way towards the nearest gangway amidships. Richard led them aft until they were standing behind an air vent, one of two only a few feet from the aftermost part of the ship's rail at the stern, one to port and one to starboard.

Alongside and outboard of each air vent there was a lifeboat. Unlike the other lifeboats, which were suspended above the ship's rail, these boats were set into a recess in the deck, and occupied a break in the rail. Along each side of the recess there was a coaming which reached almost up to the lifeboat's hull. Richard's hiding place was in the recess underneath the lifeboat. After a quick look round, Richard led them across to the other air vent on the starboard side. By ducking down under the stern of the lifeboat, he could step down into the recess, where he was almost completely hidden. Elizabeth casually looked around to see if anyone was watching, then indicated to Susan that she should follow. After another look round, Elizabeth followed. It was cramped in the recess, especially for an adult, and one encumbered with a suitcase, but as Richard had said, it was a perfect hiding place. The outboard coaming had a gap at each end to allow the recess to drain into the scuppers. They sat in the middle of the recess, on the outboard side of the lifeboat's keel, which was quite deep and reached almost to the bottom of the recess. Where they were sitting, the coaming came up to within a couple of inches of the lifeboat's hull. The gap nevertheless gave them a good view of the quayside, including the nearest gangway.

They settled down to wait. Elizabeth whispered that they should stay absolutely quiet. From where she sat, she watched as the last of the passengers disembarked. The police officers and the railway company officials continued to stand talking on the quayside by the end of the gangway. By now the light was fading rapidly as dusk faded into twilight. It continued to snow steadily. After about twenty minutes, they heard footsteps coming towards them, crunching the snow on the deck. From where they were sitting, they couldn't see inboard of the lifeboat, but they caught glimpses of light from an electric torch. They all hunched down as best they could. It was evidently one of the crew checking that there were no passengers left on board. The man stopped by the lifeboat and briefly shone his torch over the lifeboat, and into the gap between the lifeboat hull and the inboard coaming. He didn't climb round the lifeboat to do the same on the other side, contenting himself with a flick of the torch at the lifeboat from along the ship's rail. Elizabeth and the children, on the other side of the lifeboat's deep keel, remained hidden in the recess. The footsteps then faded as the man walked on.

They continued to sit in the darkness for what seemed like an age before they heard a voice calling out: "That's it, John. Everywhere's been checked. It's all clear."

A couple of minutes later, they heard the sound of the gangways being pulled away from the ship's side. The murmur of voices from the quayside persisted for a few minutes, and then there was silence. Elizabeth waited. As soon as she dared, she turned and looked through the gap above the coaming. It was now dark, but the snow on the quayside meant that it wasn't too difficult to see if anyone was standing there. As far as she could see, the quayside was now deserted. After surveying the scene for several more minutes, she decided to make a move.

"It looks as if the coast is clear," she whispered to the children. "I'm going to climb out for a better look. If it's clear, I'll tell you to come out. Remember to bring the suitcase."

Slowly, Elizabeth climbed up out of the recess and stood on the deck, with one hand on the lifeboat. After a minute looking around, she confirmed that there was no-one in the immediate vicinity on the quayside, so she whispered to the children to come out. Susan came first. Richard pushed the suitcase out before climbing out himself. Elizabeth looked over the side of the ship. Where they were standing, the hull was curving away from the quayside towards the stern, so they made their way cautiously round the lifeboat and along the rail to where the side of the ship was almost against the quayside. There was a drop of about three feet from the edge of the deck to the quayside. After another look round, Elizabeth climbed over the rail and stood right on the edge. After nerving herself and judging the distance, she jumped down. One foot slipped in the snow as she landed, and she ended up on her bottom, but she was otherwise unhurt. She got to her feet and turned towards the rail.

"Susan next," she whispered. "I'll lift you down."

Susan climbed over the rail and stood on the edge of the deck. Elizabeth reached up and lifted her down. Richard then climbed over the rail, lugging the suitcase with him, which he placed on the edge of the deck. In a display of bravado, he then jumped down himself, although he also slipped and ended up on his bottom. He quickly scrambled to his feet. Elizabeth reached up and retrieved the suitcase.

Richard reached out to Elizabeth and whispered: "Mrs Lacey – I think I've seen a way out. I saw it when we were on the top deck while there was still enough light to see. If you follow me, I'll show you."

Elizabeth was still not sure how they could get through the security fence which surrounded the harbour area, so if Richard had seen a way, that was their best bet. Where they were standing was a part of the quay which projected out into the harbour. Richard led them along the quay to the point where it joined the north wall of the harbour at right angles. He then turned and started making his way along the north wall. What he had seen previously was that the main security fence only came so far along the north wall before turning and projecting out beyond the wall for a short distance. Along the rest of the north wall, up to the quay, there were only low railings. There was a drop of about six feet from the top of the wall to a stretch of shingle at the base of the wall. What Richard had noticed was that at one point the shingle had banked up so that the drop was less than three feet. When they reached that point, he stopped.

He turned to Elizabeth and whispered: "We can jump down here. I think it's only about three feet."

Elizabeth had a look. The shingle was covered with a dusting of snow, so it was possible to estimate the distance.

"Right, I'm going to have a go," she whispered.

She climbed over the railings, steadied herself on the edge for a moment, and then jumped down. The shingle was hard and uneven, and jarred her legs as she landed; but she kept her balance and remained on her feet. She turned and helped Susan down. As before, Richard jumped down. With the suitcase retrieved, they started to make their way along the shingle at the base of the wall. Walking over the shingle produced what sounded like an alarming level of noise.

"Take your time, and try to make as little noise as possible," Elizabeth whispered.

They made their way slowly round the end of the security fence projecting out from the harbour wall. Beyond, the level of the shingle gradually rose until it was level with the top of the wall. Where the wall ended, the security fence above it turned inland, and they were able to climb up over a strip of grass and onto a road. The road continued along the shore, but after a couple of hundred yards or so it turned inland. They continued walking until the road ended in a T junction. Elizabeth didn't know Larne too well, but she had a vague idea where they were, and turned right at the junction. Her decision was confirmed when, a few minutes later, they found themselves walking along Larne's Main Street. Some shops were evidently still open, and Elizabeth decided to risk going into a newsagent, telling the children to wait outside. Her main motive in doing so was to see if she could catch a glimpse of some of the newspaper front pages, to see if any of them were carrying pictures of the children. Inside the shop, the newspapers were on a rack opposite the counter. A quick scan indicated that none of the papers had published pictures of the children. She decided to buy one of the national dailies, and had just picked a copy up when something else caught her eye. It was a book of town plans of all the main towns in Northern Ireland which, when she examined it, also included a road map of Northern Ireland.

It was a lucky find. She had a quick look at the town plan of Larne to get her bearings, then took the two items to the counter to pay for them. There was an assortment of biscuits and confectionery for sale at the counter, so she also bought a couple of packets of biscuits and a bottle of lemonade. She rejoined the children outside, and they continued along the street. At the end of the street, they turned down towards the bus station, which they reached a few minutes later.

They went into the bus station cautiously, keeping an eye open for any sign of the police. Elizabeth told the children to wait while she went into the enquiries office. She found that the next bus to Belfast was in forty minutes, so she took the children into the rather dingy waiting room. There was no heating in the room, but it was dark and cold outside, so it was better than nothing. To help pass the time, they ate some of the biscuits and drank some of the lemonade. Elizabeth had whispered to the children to speak as little as possible, to conceal their English accents.

The bus was ten minutes late. They stood huddled together with the other passengers waiting at the stand for the Belfast bus, as it continued to snow steadily. There was no sign of the police as they boarded the bus, so they boarded together, and Elizabeth bought tickets for all three of them from the conductor. After a further delay, the bus pulled out of the bus station and took the coast road down to Belfast. The snow was settling, including on the roads, which meant that the bus had to proceed slowly and cautiously. The journey to Belfast, which was scheduled for fifty-five minutes, therefore took more than an hour. The bus slowly wended its way through the streets of Belfast before finally pulling into the city's main bus station.

They climbed down from the bus into snow that was already nearly two inches deep. The snow was heavier than ever. With other passengers, they made their way towards the enquiries office. Outside, Elizabeth told the children to wait while she went inside. On entering the enquiries office, almost the first thing she saw was a policeman standing talking to the clerk behind the counter. She froze with fear. She had intended going up to the counter to ask for information. For a moment, she did not know what to do. Instinctively she turned away from the counter. As it happened, there was an information notice board and racks of leaflets with timetables for the various bus services. She quickly scanned the notice board to find the stand for the bus to Newry. As she did so, the policeman walked past her and out through the door. She experienced a moment of terror. The children were outside, only a short distance away. She had intended to get a leaflet for the service to Newry; but her only thought now was for the children. She went outside and walked over to where she had left the children. There was no sign of them. They were gone. The shock was as great as if she had been physically kicked in the stomach. To have come so far, only to face this. She almost cried out in grief. Why had she been so foolish as to leave the children? She raised a hand, trembling, to her mouth.

But at that moment, there was a hoarse whisper from the darkness.

"Mrs Lacey! Mrs Lacey!"

It was Richard. Now she did cry out, as she went towards the sound. Both the children were there, hiding behind a low wall. She hugged them and held them close, unable to stop the tears.

"Oh, I thought…"

"We saw the policeman, so we hid," whispered Richard. "He didn't see us."

"Oh, thank God."

Her mind was still in turmoil. She remained holding them for a minute, not knowing what to do. She couldn't bear to leave them again; but she knew she needed that leaflet. Eventually she said: "Stay hidden here. I need to go back and get a leaflet. I will be one minute. Keep well down behind this wall."

She stood up, and after looking around, she went back to the enquiries office. She was counting the seconds in her mind, and would not allow herself more than one minute. Inside the office, there was now no sign of the police. The clerk was dealing with an enquiry, so she quickly turned and scanned the rack of leaflets. She found the leaflet for the service to Newry, snatched a copy, and went back outside. A few seconds later, she was back with the children. She crouched down beside them behind the wall. She needed to look at the timetable. She opened her suitcase and rummaged inside it until she found the torch. She pushed the leaflet inside the suitcase and opened it, then nearly closed the lid of the suitcase before switching the torch on. Peering through the gap beneath the lid, she examined the timetable. The next bus to Newry was in seven minutes' time. Elizabeth switched the torch off and closed the suitcase. She cautiously looked over the wall before standing up.

"Right, we've got seven minutes," she whispered. "Walk together on my left-hand side." They walked over to the line of bus stands and began to walk along them. The Newry bus was at Stand G. There was a bus at Stand D, which passengers were boarding, and as they approached it, Elizabeth saw with a shock that there was a policeman with a torch checking the passengers as they boarded. There could be little doubt about the reason. Instinctively she put her arm out and drew the children to her.

"Stay close," she whispered. The children pressed themselves against her left side. They had also seen the policeman. The bus stand was on Elizabeth's right, and her heart was in her mouth as they passed within a few yards of the policeman. As she passed the bus, she glanced up at its destination board. It said 'Dublin'. They walked on until they were approaching Stand G. There was a bus waiting there with its passenger door open. There was no-one outside the bus, so Elizabeth approached the door. She pressed the children against the side of the bus, out of sight of the driver, and stepped up onto the first of the entrance steps.

"Newry?" she asked. She put on a slight Irish accent.

The driver nodded.

"Most people are going on the Dublin bus – Stand D. It leaves after this one, but it's faster, so it'll get to Newry before this one."

"Is it the same fare?"

"No, it's an extra one and three to Newry. It's an express service."

"We'll stick with this one."

As she was talking she had looked along the inside of the bus. There were a few passengers already seated, and also the conductor, who was sitting behind the driver, but no sign of the police. The indication was that the police were checking the Dublin bus because it was going to cross the border. They boarded the bus and took seats near the back of the bus. They all sat on the same seat, with the children next to the window. She whispered very quietly to each of them: "Get ready to duck down if the police board the bus."

She unfastened her coat, getting ready to take it off and spread it over the children if the police did come on board. They sat and waited. Would their luck hold? A couple of minutes later the driver started the engine, and after letting it run for a minute, he closed the passenger door and reversed the bus slowly away from the bus stand. A few minutes later they were on the A1, going through the southwestern suburbs of Belfast.

It was a journey which seemed never-ending. As the bus made its way south-west and then south across County Down, the snow got steadily thicker, as they could see through the driver's windscreen, with the headlamps illuminating a veritable blizzard of driving white flakes. In places the bus slipped and skidded as the wheels lost traction in the snow, and it was often down to little more than ten miles an hour. Elizabeth wondered if they were going to make it to Newry, as the bus reached each town along the way with grim slowness: Hillsborough, Dromore, Banbridge, Loughbrickland. The driver was clearly fighting against the elements, and she prayed that he could keep going.

At one point the bus skidded in the snow and ended up part-way off the road. At first the back wheels could gain no traction in the snow, and it looked as if they were stuck. On the fourth attempt, by slipping the clutch, the driver managed to get enough traction to move the bus back onto the road. Slowly they continued, with visibility getting steadily worse as the snow thickened. Eventually, Elizabeth saw that they had reached the outskirts of Newry. She went forward and asked the driver if he could let them off at the Downshire Road stop. He nodded, and she went back to collect the children. It was possible that the police might be checking passengers at Newry bus station. Getting off at Downshire Road would avoid that danger at least.

The bus slowed and came to a halt at the Downshire Road stop. The driver opened the passenger door. Elizabeth thanked him warmly before they climbed down the steps and out into the snow. They watched as the bus slowly moved off down the road, its red tail lamps being the last they saw of it amid the swirling snow.

"Now, we've got a long walk ahead of us," said Elizabeth. "But we have to reach the border before we will be safe. It's about five miles – that's about the same as from Ridgewell to Halstead." That would give them an idea of the distance, at least. It would be a long walk in any event, especially for Susan; but in the darkness, cold and snow…

They set off along Downshire Road, following it until it curved round into the town centre. Whilst they had been on the bus, Elizabeth had studied the book of town plans and maps by the light of her torch under her coat, so she had a fairly good idea in her head of their route. The snow was now three or four inches deep, so they had to plough through it, which slowed their progress. In the town centre, they crossed the bridge over the river. At the far end of the bridge they turned left onto the road that ran alongside the Newry River. This was the road that led to the border.

For the first few hundred yards, there were houses and other buildings along the right-hand side of the road, before these eventually gave way to the hedges, trees and fields of open countryside. Along the left-hand side of the road, and more or less constantly in view, was the Newry River, its dark expanse contrasting with the snowy landscape, even at night. It continued to snow as heavily as ever, and it was steadily settling and building up. It wasn't long before they were ploughing through snow at least six inches deep; and in places they encountered drifts of snow more than a foot deep.

At first, the children found walking through the snow fun, and from time to time they would kick up the snow in front of them as they walked. Gradually, however, as one seemingly endless mile followed another, the novelty wore off, and they eventually lapsed into silence as they ploughed on through the ever-thicker snow.

At length, Susan asked plaintively: "Is it much farther to go?"

In truth, Elizabeth was not sure. She suspected that they had not walked as far as they might have thought, because of the difficulty of ploughing through the snow; but she needed to encourage them to keep going. The only reference point she had was that, according to the map, the river swung away from the road to the left at the border. Thus far, the river had been more or less continuously in view.

"I think we're more than half-way there now. Perhaps another twenty minutes to go," she said, trying to sound as encouraging as possible.

But after twenty minutes there was still no sign that they had reached their objective. At one point, they lost sight of the river behind an increasingly dense bank of trees along the left-hand side of the road, leading Elizabeth to think that they may have reached the point where the river parted from the road; but after a couple of hundred yards the river was suddenly back on the left-hand side of the road. It was evidently just a point where the riverbank projected out into the river for a short distance. Slowly they went on; but Elizabeth sensed that Susan was in difficulty.

Eventually, Susan said: "I don't know if I can go on for much longer, Mrs Lacey. I'm so tired and cold."

Elizabeth was alarmed at this. If Susan's endurance gave out, what could she do?

"We have to keep going, love, or we'll freeze to death. We can stop and rest for a few minutes if you like."

"Yes, alright."

They stopped and sat down in the snow. The falling snow whirled around them as they sat.

"Shall I go on ahead and see if I can see anything?" asked Richard.

"No, we must stay together," said Elizabeth, experiencing a new alarm. "You might never find us again in this snow."

After a few minutes, Susan said she was ready to try again, and they began to walk slowly forward again. But it wasn't long before Susan requested another stop, and again they sat down and rested for a few minutes before continuing. This happened several times, and Elizabeth noted that the intervals between rests were getting shorter. Susan was reaching the limits of her endurance. Elizabeth didn't know what she would do when that point was reached, and it obviously wouldn't be long now. Perhaps she would have to let Richard go on ahead if he could, to try and see how much farther they had to go. In fact, Richard was already a little distance ahead, as Elizabeth stayed with Susan, whose strength was nearly gone.

He suddenly called out to them: "I can see a light ahead!" He waited while they came up to him. They had reached a bend in the road, and the trees were suddenly dense on the left-hand side of the road, with no sign of the river. There was indeed a light ahead, perhaps 150 yards away.

"I think we're almost there," said Elizabeth. "Come on, let's go and see," she said encouragingly to Susan.

Slowly, painfully slowly now, they ploughed on through the snow. The light was from the lighted windows of a house, on the right-hand side of the road. As they came up to it, Elizabeth saw that it was a pub or an inn. Wherever they were, they could go no farther that night.

It was a quarter to ten – the inn was still open. Elizabeth told the children to stand against the wall of the inn near the door, while she went inside.

"I need to check what the situation is first," she said.

Inside, the inn was warm, and even the dim lighting of the bar seemed bright after the darkness outside. The air was laden with the aromas of beer and cigarette smoke as a few late drinkers finished their drinks. There was a peat fire glowing in the fireplace. Everyone looked at Elizabeth as she came in.

"I'm afraid I've got lost on the road," she said to the man behind the bar. "Can you tell me where I am?"

"Where are you headed?" he asked.

"Carlingford," she said.

"Carlingford? That's a few miles on from here. It's not good to be walking such a distance in weather like this."

That Elizabeth had been walking was evidenced by the snow on her coat and shoes.

"Where is this?" she asked.

"This is Cornamucklagh," he said.

Elizabeth couldn't remember seeing that name on the map.

"Cornamucklagh, County Armagh?"

"No, Cornamucklagh, County Louth. We're in County Louth here."

"County Louth? Then we've made it! We've made it! Oh, thank God!"

"There's someone with you?"

"I have two children outside. Could you put us up for the night?"

"Yes, we have a room to spare. I don't think it would be a good idea to try and reach Carlingford tonight in this snow."

"I'll just go and bring the children in."

She went out to where the children were waiting. She put her arms round them both and hugged them to her.

"We've made it! We've crossed the border! This is County Louth. We're safe! We're safe at last!"

She led them inside. They were all cold, exhausted and famished. Susan had reached the limits of her endurance. But the ordeal was over now. Chairs were found for them by the fireplace, where they were able to take off wet and snow-laden coats and stretch out to the restorative warmth of the peat fire. Hot drinks were brought, and then food. Soon there would be a bed to give them rest and sleep. Tomorrow, she could plan their return to Dublin, free from fear. They were safe. She could look forward with confidence, for the first time, to the homecoming at the big house on Cambridge Road, where they were all waiting for her and the children; to seeing them all again; to seeing the children in their new home for the first time.

And Mike…

Carl Richardson
30th November 2019